P9-ARU-136

TAKEN

Also by Lisa Harris and available from
Center Point Large Print:

Dangerous Passage
Hidden Agenda

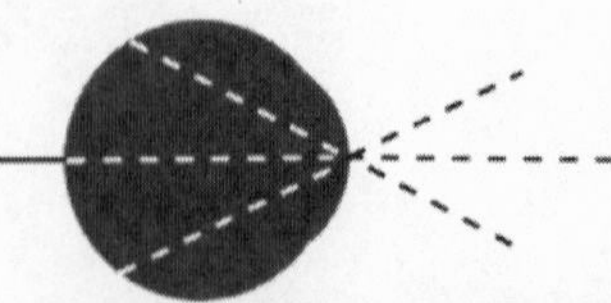

This Large Print Book carries the
Seal of Approval of N.A.V.H.

TAKEN

LISA
HARRIS

CENTER POINT LARGE PRINT
THORNDIKE, MAINE

This Center Point Large Print edition is published in the year 2015 by arrangement with Harlequin Books S.A.

The text of this Large Print edition is unabridged.
In other aspects, this book may vary
from the original edition.
Printed in the United States of America
on permanent paper.
Set in 16-point Times New Roman type.

ISBN: 978-1-62899-691-3

Library of Congress Cataloging-in-Publication Data

Harris, Lisa, 1969–
Taken / Lisa Harris. — Center Point Large Print edition.
pages cm
Summary: "Kate Elliot's suburban life turns upside down when her sister is shot and her niece kidnapped. FBI agent Marcus O'Brian is investigating a diamond smuggling case that he thinks is connected to the kidnapping. When Kate follows a lead to Paris, she finds herself in danger and she and Marcus join forces"—Provided by publisher.
ISBN 978-1-62899-691-3 (library binding : alk. paper)
1. Kidnapping—Fiction.
2. United States. Federal Bureau of Investigation—Fiction.
3. Large type books.
I. Title.
PS3608.A78315T35 2015
813′.6—dc23

2015021113

Dedicated to my husband
and all of our fun memories
of the most romantic city in the world.

If I go up to the heavens, you are there; if I make my bed in the depths, you are there. If I rise on the wings of the dawn, if I settle on the far side of the sea, even there your hand will guide me, your right hand will hold me fast.

—*Psalms* 139:8–10

TAKEN

ONE

"Nine-one-one, what's your emergency?"

Kate Elliot pressed her cell phone against her ear with her shoulder as she fumbled to open her sister's front door with her spare key. The lock stuck. "My sister . . . I think . . . I think she's been shot."

"What is the location of the emergency, ma'am?"

Kate squeezed her eyes shut, fighting back tears as she gave the woman her sister's address.

"The paramedics are en route now, ma'am."

Thirty seconds later, Kate managed to open the door. She stepped inside the two-story house in the upscale Dallas suburb, her heart pounding. Dora the Explorer giggled on the flat-screen TV in the living room. The normally immaculate house had been completely trashed.

"Rachel!" She screamed out her sister's name.

Kate picked up the remote, froze Dora's character, then called for her sister again, but only an eerie silence greeted her. Trying not to panic, she checked quickly through the down-stairs.

There was no sign of her sister.

She headed up the stairs straight for the master bedroom. Like the rest of the house, the room had been trashed. Bedding lay in mounds on the floor, framed photos had been ripped off the walls and dresser drawers dumped onto the floor. Their contents lay strewn across the bloodstained carpet—all telltale signs of the horror that had taken place moments before.

Rachel lay still on her back in the middle of the room.

Kate dropped to her knees beside her sister, avoiding a thick shard of glass from a broken mirror, and grasped Rachel's wrist. The monotone beeping from the receiver of the landline vied for attention against a pulse that was steady but weak.

Rachel groaned and opened her eyes.

"Don't move, sweetie. I'm here." Fighting back the tears, Kate wiped off the perspiration that had beaded across Rachel's ashen forehead.

"They broke in through the back door . . . They had guns . . . It all happened so fast . . ."

"An ambulance is almost here, and they'll get you to the hospital. You're going to be okay, Rachel. I promise."

Kate's gaze shot to her sister's bloodstained dress and realized it was a promise she might not be able to keep. "Rachel, stay with me. Please."

Grabbing a bathrobe off the floor, Kate pressed the fuzzy garment against Rachel's abdomen where the bullet had entered. The white material immediately took on a deep crimson stain.

Oh, God, please don't take her now. Not this way.

Rachel's eyes widened as she gasped for air. "Sophie . . . They took Sophie."

"Sophie's fine, honey. She's with Mom." Kate forced her voice to stay calm despite the sick feeling spreading through her. Rachel had to be mistaken. Sophie spent every Monday, Wednesday and Friday morning with Grams. And today was Monday.

But if that was true, why had *Dora* been on?

Rachel's mouth twisted from the pain. "No . . . Mom couldn't keep her today. Her arthritis is flaring up again."

The walls of Kate's stomach contracted. Surely someone hadn't taken her four-year-old niece. She brushed back a strand of Rachel's auburn hair. "I didn't see her when I came in, but if she's not with Mom, she has to be here somewhere."

Kate glanced at the open door of the bedroom, trying not to imagine what Sophie might have seen. Armed men breaking in and tearing apart the house. Her mother shot. And if they *had* taken her . . .

"Sophie?" she shouted. "Are you here, sweetie? It's Auntie Kate."

No response.

Kate pressed harder against Rachel's wound to try to stop the bleeding, as her mind scrambled to put together a time line. She'd arrived moments after Rachel's call, unclear from her sister's frantic speech as to what had happened, other than the chilling words that she'd been shot.

They shot me, Kit Kat. Hurry . . . please. I can't . . .

The moment she'd stepped into her sister's house, it had been clear that something was terribly wrong. Someone had been here, systematically going through every inch of the house. Looking for something. But what?

The tug to find Sophie grew stronger, but for now, she had no choice but to stay with her sister.

"Rachel, I need you to try to focus for a minute. Who shot you?"

Rachel's gaze narrowed. "Two men."

Kate listened for signs that someone was still in the house, while trying to swallow the terror. "Do you know them?"

Rachel shook her head.

"What about Sophie?"

"They took her." A shriek erupted from Rachel's lips as she fought to sit up. "I know they did. They took my baby."

Kate held Rachel tighter. She had to be mistaken. "Sophie has to be here. What reason would anyone have to take her?"

Rachel's breathing grew raspier. "I don't know."

Kate glanced at the window. Where was the ambulance?

"You have to know something, Rachel. They

were here, looking for something. What were they looking for?"

"I said I don't know."

Kate frowned. If Sophie was missing—and Rachel didn't make it—they were going to need every clue possible to find her. "Try to think. Please. Does this have anything to do with Chad?"

She'd never known Rachel's husband to be abusive, but that didn't mean their marriage had always been amiable.

Kate remembered that Saturday Rachel had met her for lunch and told her not only that she was pregnant, but that she was going to marry the baby's father. Rachel had spent that summer in Europe, traveling with a group of friends, and had fallen for the first Frenchman who'd caught her eye. Kate might not have approved of the relationship, but she'd seen the love Rachel had for Chad and prayed that they'd find a way to make it work. They'd all hoped for happily-ever-after. But sometimes life didn't turn out that way.

"When I went to see him . . . in Paris . . . he told me he was scared." Rachel choked out the words. "He told me they would do anything to . . . to get what they wanted."

Kate tried to put together the pieces. Rachel had left for Paris three months ago to try to patch up her relationship with her husband, Chad. When she returned, Rachel had distanced herself, never opening up about the trip. Kate had assumed her silence was her way to deal with her failing marriage. Now she realized it had to be much more than that. She'd always feared Chad and Rachel's relationship might one day end in divorce. She'd worried about how Sophie would handle the loss of a father, and how Rachel would cope as a single mom, but she'd never considered the scenario they were facing now. Not the reality of her sister fighting for her life.

"Who are they?" Kate asked. "What do they want?"

Sirens screamed in the distance.

"I think he's involved in something illegal," Rachel said.

"What?"

"He wouldn't tell me."

"Did Chad take Sophie?"

"No, but it could be . . . someone he's involved with."

Flashing lights from the ambulance reflected against the beige walls of the bedroom. Kate heard the front door slam against the foyer wall and shouted to the paramedics to come upstairs.

Rachel gripped Kate's forearm. "Promise . . . promise me you'll find her, Kate. Don't let anything happen to her. Please . . . please, Kate . . . she's all I have."

Kate nodded at her sister. "You know I'll do everything I can. I promise."

The following minutes clicked by like a hazy fog.

Kate stood at the edges of the room, watching the paramedics try to stabilize Rachel. She'd already explained to one of the officers that not only had her sister been shot, but her niece was missing. The room tilted as they searched the house for Sophie. Nausea spread through her. Nothing made sense. Rachel was a mom who worked part-time as a hairdresser at a local beauty shop. Someone clearly wanted something that was worth killing for, but what? And why would they take Sophie?

Thirty minutes later, Kate stood in the waiting room while doctors rushed to save Rachel's life.

As she leaned against one of the walls, an officer approached her and began peppering her with questions. Though sympathetic, he wanted answers—fast. Did she know who had shot her sister? Did she know where her niece was?

Kate caught the young officer's gaze, fighting the urge to scream. No. She didn't have any answers. Didn't know who had shot Rachel. Didn't know where Sophie was.

As he continued to ask her questions she had no clue how to answer, she thought about calling her mother and the pastor from their church, but had no idea what to say. How was she supposed to break the news to her mother that Rachel might be dying and Sophie was missing?

She wondered if they should expect a ransom note. That was how they did it on television. Cops or FBI agents waited with the grieving family until the kidnappers called to make their demands. They needed to find out what they were after, and if this were somehow connected to Chad, because Rachel didn't have the kind of money kidnappers would demand.

Which meant she needed to talk with Chad. She tried his preprogrammed number she'd kept on her phone. No answer. Despite their failing marriage, Kate couldn't imagine the man shooting Rachel and leaving her for dead. The two might have had their issues, but she didn't think Chad was capable of murder—or even kidnapping, for that matter.

Except all the signs were there. Possible divorce, a string of heated arguments, and if he was involved in something illegal . . . Even if he hadn't been here, Chad had to know something.

She punched in his number again, wondering what time it was in Paris right now. Wondering why he wasn't answering.

Only one thing was clear at the moment. She was going to keep her promise to her sister and find Sophie.

Monday afternoon, Marcus O'Brian slid the key into the front door of the upscale house and slipped past the yellow tape. Operation Solitaire had turned into a yearlong investigation with diamonds being smuggled into the United States in exchange for military-grade weapons for a number of third-world African countries. And his search had led him here.

After weeks of dead ends, he still had more questions than answers. Which was why coming here was a long shot, but it wasn't one he was willing to dismiss. Chad Laurent, half French, half American, might be working as a legitimate buyer for an international jewelry company, but now Marcus had compelling evidence Chad was buying and selling diamonds sourced from illegitimate channels; uncertified diamonds that had been smuggled into the international market and in turn sold as legitimate gems. And now on top of that, the man was a prime suspect in an attempted murder case and kidnapping charges of his wife and daughter.

He stepped through the front door and studied the layout of the three-bedroom, two-story house that had been ransacked—open-concept living room, dining room and kitchen, with a wide staircase to the second floor. Among the chaos were picture books, puzzles, stacks of children's DVDs and colorful drawings hanging on the fridge. He went over in his mind everything he knew about Rachel Elliot Laurent. Married for five years, but currently separated from her husband. There was no evidence of abuse, which was why the shooting seemed out of character if Chad was behind it. Or at least unexpected. But the rules of the game had changed, and he had a feeling that Rachel wasn't as innocent as she'd portrayed herself to be in their interview three days before the shooting.

Something about her demeanor had rubbed him the wrong way. She'd insisted she knew nothing about Chad's possible illegal activities, especially now that her husband had relocated to Paris six months ago, but she'd been hiding something. He was certain of it.

He heard a noise upstairs. Marcus's pulse shot up a notch. Someone else was in the house. He took the stairs to the second floor slowly, gun drawn, senses alert to the unfamiliar sounds of the house. According to his contact within the local PD, no one should be here. More than likely it was someone who'd decided to take advantage of the empty house, or a family member who didn't care that this was a crime scene. If he were lucky, the perpetrator had returned to the scene of the crime.

He stepped through the doorway of the master bedroom and stopped. A woman knelt beside an open wooden chest facing away from him, going through the contents. Like the rest of the house, the room had been trashed, but here, blood stained the light-colored carpet. The crime scene unit had already swept the house for evidence, but whoever she was, she clearly wasn't supposed to be here.

"I want you to put your hands in the air and stand up slowly." He held his weapon level and aimed it at her as she stood and turned toward him, clearly alarmed by his presence.

"Who are you?" she asked as she followed his instructions.

"I could ask you the same thing." He took a step toward her. Recognition skirted his memory as he searched for a name. "Kate Elliot?"

Her frown deepened. "How do you know my name?"

"I know your sister. Wow. The two of you could be twins."

"Irish twins, actually. We were born eleven months apart. But that doesn't answer the question of what you're doing here."

He stopped midstride, and pulled back the front of his black tailored sports coat. "My name is Marcus O'Brian. I'm with the FBI, investigating what happened to your sister."

He studied her briefly—shoulder-length, reddish- blond hair pulled up in a ponytail, intense hazel-colored eyes. Something struck him about the intensity of her posture, like a mama bear defending her cubs. But why not? Her sister had been shot and her niece was missing. And from her defiant expression, she didn't believe he was one of the good guys.

"Why is the FBI involved?" she asked.

He lowered his weapon and reholstered it. He didn't have evidence that Rachel was involved in her husband's illegal activities, but that didn't mean he wasn't going to keep digging. "I can't talk about that."

"Do you know who shot her?"

"No . . . but I am sorry." He knew she was hurting, but showing empathy had never been his strong point. "How is she?"

"She came out of surgery, but she's still unconscious. And the last I heard there were still no firm leads on my niece's whereabouts."

"Were you here when she was shot?"

"No, but I was on my way. I found her here. Whoever shot her took Sophie and left Rachel to bleed to death."

"Do you have any idea who might have wanted to hurt her?" he asked.

"No. I've already told the police everything I do know, which isn't much."

"Like I said, I'm not with the police."

"Don't you share information?"

"Yes, but I'm in the middle of a separate investigation connected to her husband."

"Chad?" The fatigue in her eyes deepened. "Do you think Chad is behind my sister getting shot?"

"At this point, I have no idea. What I do know is that the FBI is currently investigating Chad for possible involvement in an open criminal case where your sister is a potential witness." Or in his mind, a suspect, but he wasn't going to bring that up at this time. "Do you think it's possible your brother-in-law was involved in the shooting?"

"At this point, I'd believe almost anything, but I don't think so. Chad can be a jerk, but he doesn't like to get his hands dirty. And besides, I can't see him shooting Rachel, or taking Sophie, for that matter. He threatened to get a divorce once or twice, but as far as I know he's never moved ahead with his threats. He wants to see Sophie, without the responsibility of raising her. Bottom line is I can't see the point of him snatching her."

"So what do you know?"

"I know that someone broke into this house looking for something." Her gaze dropped as she fiddled with a loose thread on the edge of her purple T-shirt. Tense. Nervous. "I know that my sister is lying in ICU and my niece is gone. I know I probably shouldn't be here, but I thought I might find some clue of what Rachel—and Chad—are mixed up in."

He studied her expression. There was something she wasn't telling him. "Do you know what they're mixed up in?"

"No, but someone was clearly looking for something and I want to know what."

Something unexpected triggered inside him as her expression softened. She might appear strong on the surface, but she was also clearly vulnerable. A part of him wanted to sweep her out of here and protect her from whatever she'd innocently walked into. Which was crazy. One, he had no idea if she really was innocent. And two, his job was to take down criminals, not simply to rescue pretty damsels in distress.

Marcus shoved aside the unexpected attraction. He'd watched his own family struggle to balance the stress of a career in law enforcement with relationships and too many of them hadn't survived. Those who did, carried their own scars that he wanted nothing to do with. Nicole had managed to substantiate that conclusion when she forced him to choose between her and his career.

He shook his head at the unwanted memory. He needed to stay on track. "Has your sister traveled recently?"

Kate closed the lid of the trunk and sat down on it. "She went to Paris three months ago. I've been looking through her photos and journals to see if something happened there that might give me a clue as to what Chad might be involved in—or any suspicions she might have had—but so far, I can't find anything out of the ordinary, except for one thing . . ."

"What is it?"

"It's probably nothing, but I can't find her passport, which is strange. Rachel's very compulsive and orderly. She's going to have a fit trying to put this house back together."

"Where does she normally keep the passport?"

"At one time she kept it in this trunk, where she keeps a lot of her important papers like birth certificates and financial papers. She probably just moved it."

"Do you think she's involved with something illegal?" he asked.

"Rachel? Never."

But he'd seen Rachel's financials and knew her credit cards were maxed out and she was behind on her house payments. Money could be a powerful motivator. Which was why he couldn't dismiss the possibility of her being involved in what happened today. Or that Kate Elliot knew more than she was letting on.

Kate stood up and started past the red stain on the carpet. Nausea swept through her. The room smelled like death and she needed some fresh air. "I need to return to the hospital. If I don't take my mother home, she'll stay there all night."

"Wait . . . before you go, I need to ask you a few questions. It won't take long. I promise."

She hesitated, then reluctantly sat back down on the edge of the trunk. She was tired. Tired of the questions that she didn't have answers for. Tired of waiting on an update from the hospital. Afraid of the panic that had yet to lessen. And this man, Marcus O'Brian, was simply adding to that panic.

"You and your sister are close?" he began.

"For the most part, yes."

"What about Chad? How was their relationship?"

"That was a subject we didn't talk about often.

I didn't think he was good enough for her and she resented that. So we avoided the subject."

"Why didn't you think he was good enough for her?"

Kate hesitated, wondering how her sister's marital relationship was going to help find her shooter. She might not have thought he was the best choice for her sister to marry, but Rachel loved him and he was the father of their child.

"Please understand," Marcus continued. "I realize I'm probing into something very personal, but the more I know about Chad and your sister, the easier it will be for me to find out the truth as to who was behind this. And for now, I can't go to her with my questions."

Kate let out a sharp sigh. "It bothered me that he put his job above his family. He traveled a lot, which meant he was gone more than he was home, something I know she resented. Especially because of Sophie."

"Where did his job take him?"

"They have an apartment in Paris. He worked in both the US and Europe as a buyer. Occasionally he traveled to Africa."

"And his traveling took a toll on their marriage?"

"It was more than just the traveling, but yes. Six months ago, he moved back to Paris. I think divorce was on the table, but there wasn't anything official."

"Did they still communicate?"

"Some. My sister went to Paris three months ago to try to see if they could give their marriage one last chance."

"And when she returned, what did she tell you about the trip?"

"Not much, but it was clear that it didn't go the way she'd hoped. I think she still loved him—that she still does—but it became clear to her that he had no intentions of settling down and giving her what she wanted." Her gaze dropped to the stained spot on the carpet.

"What is it?"

Kate grabbed one of the throw pillows off the bed and hugged it against her chest, wishing he wasn't able to read her so well. "While we were waiting for the ambulance, she told me Chad was scared about something."

"About what?"

"I don't know. All Rachel said was that they would do anything to get what they wanted." She looked up at him, the fear she'd been feeling all day gripping her tighter. "Do you know what Chad's involved in?"

"Let me ask the questions for now. Later, I'll answer those that aren't classified."

"Classified." Kate shook her head, irritation weaving itself through the fear. "You sound like James Bond."

"No. Real life doesn't play out like the movies."

No, it didn't. And today had become an extreme example. One couldn't simply go home once the credits rolled.

"Do you think Rachel knew what he was involved in?" he asked.

She tried not to show her resentment of the question. "No."

Marcus took a step forward. "Did she ever mention being suspicious about his behavior?"

Kate shook her head. "You have to understand that I want to help, but there is nothing I can tell you that is going to help us find Sophie and my sister's shooter. We need to talk to Chad. He's got to know—"

"We?" Marcus shook his head. "What you need to do is let the police—and myself—handle this. We are looking for him right now, in fact, and when we find him, we'll interview him. But you're not a part of *we*."

"But I know Chad."

"And I know what happens when civilians try to get involved in police business. Trust me, it doesn't work."

"So you haven't been able to locate Chad yet?"

He hesitated. "No."

"Then what about Sophie?" she rushed on. "You have to know something. Have some lead as to where she might be. Sophie, she's . . . she's four years old, full of energy and has the biggest imagination I've ever seen. She's silly and loves to tell jokes—"

"Kate—"

"She loves macaroni from the box and strawberry licorice," Kate continued, as if she were pleading her case in court. She might sound desperate, but needed him to realize this wasn't just some missing person, or some domestic dispute in another case he was working on. "Sophie loves Dora the Explorer, going to Sunday school. She can't sleep without her one-eyed bunny, Lily."

Marcus's eyes widened. "I don't have an update about your niece, except . . ."

"What do you know?" she prodded.

"You told me your sister's passport was missing."

"Sophie's has to be missing, as well."

"We checked airline manifest lists since her father lives in France." Hands clenched at her sides, she waited for him to continue. "Both passports were used to fly to Paris. A woman and a little girl, presumably your niece."

A ball of emotion tangled inside Kate as she fought not to cry. "So Sophie's in Paris?"

"That's what we believe."

Chad was AWOL . . . Sophie was missing . . .

Kate pressed her lips together, because at the moment, there only seemed to be one solution. No matter what Marcus O'Brian, with his perfect profile and piercing blue eyes, had said, she'd already made up her mind. There was only one person in her mind who had the answers. She needed to talk to Chad. Even if that meant flying to Paris and finding Chad herself.

Two

At nine twenty-nine Wednesday morning, Central European time, Kate was already second-guessing herself and wondering—not for the first time—if flying halfway around the world had been a sane decision.

She clutched the strap of her pink tote bag and pressed through the crowded promenade running parallel to the famous Champs Elysées. Lined with boutiques, chic restaurants and fancy storefronts, it was exactly how she'd imagined Paris. But after thirteen hours of travel, two planes, the RER train into the city and a taxi, her decision seemed impulsive, even reckless. But what choice did she have? She needed answers. Needed to speak with Chad. Needed to find Sophie. Careless or not, she was still convinced that coming to Paris had been her only option. Chad was the key to finding Sophie.

Which was why there'd been little time to think through the consequences of her actions. She'd charged the airline ticket to her credit card, booked a hotel, then pulled out everything she had on Paris in her travel files. A quick check-in at her hotel after landing, along with a shower, had helped clear her mind, but it hadn't quite managed to squelch the anxiety or the fear. Added to her list of frustrations was Marcus O'Brian, who had yet to give her an update on his investigation.

Not that he owed her one, she supposed, but a phone call from the man would go a long way. And not because he'd appeared in her dreams last night, or that she'd yet been unable to forget those blue eyes of his. She just needed someone on her side. So far the only person who'd seemed happy for her company had been the taxi driver who'd gladly exchanged her Euros for a neck-breaking race from her hotel to Chad's place of employment.

Kate glanced at her map, then scanned the stone-cut buildings beside her with their decorative ironwork, looking for Anne-Loure, the jewelry shop where Chad worked. The taxi driver had dropped her off short of the shop, but she'd wanted the exercise and hopefully time to get her bearings. But apparently, he'd left her farther from the store than she'd intended. According to her map, the shop was still a half-dozen blocks away. Exploring the famed City of Lights and its history had always been on the top ten of her bucket list. But not this way.

Paris was supposed to be savored slowly while sipping a café au lait. Lazy afternoons strolling alongside the Seine or leisurely digesting the history of a local museum. Even now, she could sense the historic city's energy. With its offering of historic sites like the Louvre, Notre Dame and the Eiffel Tower, Paris was a mecca for tourists, artists and historians.

Kate blew out a sharp breath. This wasn't exactly how she'd expected to spend her first trip to Paris. She and Kevin had decided on a twelve-day tour of Europe's cities of lights for their honeymoon, including two nights each in Paris and Prague. A scenic river cruise along the Rhine, Heidelberg . . . It would have been the perfect honeymoon until Kevin ran off and married her best friend, who would have been the maid of honor at their wedding.

She'd always thought the story would make the perfect script for a romantic comedy—if it had a different ending. Something along the lines of jilted bride finds love with lonely best man or something like that, but in her case, there had been no lonely best man or happy ending. Just a lot of embarrassment and explanations as to why her fiancé was honeymooning with her best friend.

At least she hadn't burned the contents of the honeymoon folder, because today she needed the spreadsheet with travel information, Google maps, online transportation websites, hotels and dozens of other details she'd collected and organized while planning their trip.

She was over Kevin. Their broken engagement seemed like a lifetime ago most days. And maybe now something good was going to come out of the situation. She'd traveled enough outside the United States to feel fairly confident as long as she had a map and cell phone in hand.

But as much as the city might beckon, she needed to stay focused on one thing and one thing only.

Finding Sophie.

She ran her finger across the photos of Sophie she'd stuck inside the cover of her travel guide—a reminder as to why she was here. Brown hair, bright blue eyes and a smile that melted your heart in two. This was why she was here. Because if anything happened to her—

Someone brushed against her shoulder. The hairs on her neck bristled. Kate stiffened as a long-haired teen walked away, not even acknowledging the incident. She shook off the eerie sensation. Marcus flashed through her mind, making her wish he was with her, but she quickly shoved away the image. He might have that classic tall, dark and handsome look going for him, and an overprotective vibe, too, but he was also a federal agent with an agenda. He believed Rachel was involved in something illegal. She'd seen it in his eyes, along with the suspicion toward herself. Which meant the man wasn't worth the risk of a second look.

And she didn't need him. Because no one was watching her. No one was after her. Lack of sleep, long hours of travel and the added guilt from being unable to protect her sister were messing with her mind.

But she couldn't ignore the knot of fear that had settled into the pit of her stomach. She turned and glanced behind her. How was it possible that in a sea of pedestrians, she still felt as if she were being followed? She hesitated beneath the shade of a shop awning. Notre Dame loomed a few blocks away with its stunning stained glass windows and gargoyles. For a moment, she considered running to the safety and quiet of the historic church. But God could hear her constant prayers just as well here as in the middle of a cathedral. She forced her mind to focus. Speaking with Chad was her one priority right now.

Someone's elbow jabbed her from behind. This time, her bag slipped from her shoulder and crashed to the sidewalk, its contents scattering across the pavement. She lunged for the pink MP3 player that had tumbled out and started to grab it, but the man hovering over her snatched it first.

Shaken, she stood up, hand outstretched, and caught the man's steel gaze. When he still wouldn't hand over the MP3, she chanced that he would understand English, and asked, "What do you want?"

He pulled back his jacket revealing the tip of the gun he was carrying. "I want you to come with me."

The knot in her stomach tightened. She glanced

around at the shoppers passing by. She could run, but if he caught her, she'd never be able to fight him.

She decided to scream.

Fingers dug into her arm as he dragged her toward the street. "Shut up and get in the car."

She continued screaming as he shoved her into the backseat of a waiting car. Her elbow slammed against the door frame. She couldn't think. Couldn't breathe. They'd shot Rachel . . . taken Sophie . . . What in the world did they want with her?

She scrambled across the backseat, then lunged for the handle on the opposite side. The door was unlocked. He grabbed her foot, but she jerked away from his grasp and stumbled out of the car, still managing to grip her bag. But the action threw her into traffic. Cars whizzed by. The man scooted across the seat behind her. She slammed the door on him, but the driver was climbing out of the front of the vehicle.

Kate lunged out into the path of an oncoming taxi, then swerved to the left. There was no way she could cross the busy traffic without getting hit. She ran around the back of the car toward the sidewalk, hoping to lose herself in a sea of shoppers. Brakes squealed and a taxi missed her by inches, but the near accident barely registered.

What did they want with her?

For the first time, she wished she'd listened to

Marcus. He'd been right. She should never have come. She had no business tracking down her sister's shooter on her own. All she wanted was answers and justice and to get her niece back. Instead, she'd gotten herself involved in a situation where not only were her sister's and Sophie's lives at stake, but somehow she'd become tangled up in the mess.

A flock of pigeons scattered into the air in front of her. She turned onto a side street, disoriented without the help of the map. But she couldn't take the time to pull it out. All she knew to do was to keep zigzagging through the narrow streets until she lost them. She could figure out where she was later.

Lungs screaming for air, she forced herself to keep running. She had no one to call. Nowhere to run for help. In a city of millions, she'd never felt so alone.

A car pulled up beside her. "Get in!"

Kate kept running, but something made her pause and turn. Marcus sat in the driver's seat.

"Get in the car," he repeated.

Still out of breath, Kate slid into the car and dropped her bag onto the floorboard, too scared to ask questions. Too scared to consider the fact that she might not be trusting the right person.

Marcus pressed on the accelerator as he pulled into the heavy traffic and tried to bite back his irritation. Kate Elliot was supposed to be five thousand miles away in Dallas, Texas. Not trying to track down her sister's shooter on her own here in Paris. No. From what he remembered, he'd given her specific instruction that she was to let him and the police handle the investigation of her sister's attempted murder. Flying to Paris in search of her niece—as she'd clearly done—had not been an option. But for the moment, he couldn't worry about what she'd done or why she was here. He needed to get her somewhere safe.

Marcus changed lanes and sped down the avenue, weaving in and out of traffic, hoping he'd catch sight of the vehicle that had tried to snatch her. But as much as he wanted to catch whoever had tried to grab her, for the moment her safety needed to be the priority. Because chasing down the bad guys with Kate Elliot at his side wasn't a good idea.

"Are they following us?" he asked.

She looked back. "I don't know. The cars . . . they all look the same."

"It was a dark compact—"

"They're all compact cars . . . or taxis."

"I need a description, Kate. A license plate number—something I was unable to get. We need to find those guys."

His irritation grew. They were the reason he was here. He needed to catch those guys and now he'd somehow ended up saddled with Kate and needing to think about her protection.

Which raised even more questions than he had answers. Like how did they know she'd be here in the first place?

"I was on my way to Chad's store."

"I was just there. He didn't come in to work today."

"You think they're still after us?" she asked, her voice ragged.

"I managed to find you, and I don't think they're simply going to give up. So yes. There's a good chance they're still back there."

"They had a gun . . ." Her jaw was set, determined, but she still sounded as if she were about to hyperventilate. "They shoved me into a car."

"I know. I was driving by when you came flying out of that car into the traffic. You're lucky you weren't killed. I don't know what you were thinking—"

Someone smashed into the back of his rental car, shoving both of them forward.

Marcus gripped the steering wheel as he swerved to avoid a collision with the car in front of him. "Hang on, Kate. I think we just found them."

THREE

They'd found them.

"Marcus!"

Kate could hear the edge of panic in her voice. Gripping the armrest with her fingers, she tried not to hyperventilate as the car rammed into them a second time. She winced as her head hit the side of the car. Marcus would get them out of this. He had to. And she had no choice but to trust him. They were just trying to scare them. But why? None of it made sense. They already had Sophie. What else did they want?

Please, God . . . all I want to do is find Sophie and make sure she's safe. But I don't even know what is going on.

"What do they want?" Kate spoke her question out loud, her arms braced for another impact.

"I don't know. Are you sure it's them?"

She glanced back again and caught sight of the bald head of the man who'd tried to grab her off the street. She'd recognize him anywhere. "Yes. Besides, I can't believe this is just a coincidence."

Marcus's jaw tensed, the vein in his neck pulsing, as he sped down a one-way street lined with bikes and motorcycles. Pedestrians strolled down the sidewalk, casting glances as they sped past. He slowed down as he came to a busy intersection, and managed to merge into traffic without stopping.

Kate dug her nails into the armrest, willing the car to go faster. "We need to lose them."

"Not yet. Keep your eye on them. I need a license plate."

"A license plate?" She craned her neck so she could see out the back window and squinted as she tried to read the plate. The car behind them sped forward, hitting again.

Her seat belt caught as her body snapped forward.

"You okay?" he asked.

"Yeah. I got the license." Kate scrambled for a pen then wrote down the number on her hand.

"Good, because now I need you to make a call."

"The police?"

"I'm working with French intelligence. They'll be able to get us some backup."

Her hands shook as she grabbed his phone, which was sitting between them.

Marcus kept his eyes on the road beside her, weaving in and out of traffic, with the car still on their tail. "Scroll through the favorites contacts and look for Pierre. Make the call, then put it on speakerphone so I can talk to him."

A moment later, a man with a heavy French accent answered. "Bonjour?"

"Pierre, it's Marcus."

"Did you find Chad?"

"No, but I did run into his sister-in-law."

Kate felt her fear morphing into anger as Marcus explained the situation while speeding through the heart of Paris. She glanced out the back window again. This time there was no sign of the other car.

"I'll let you know what I find out about the license plate," Pierre said.

"Good," Marcus said. "I'll meet you at the safe house in thirty minutes."

Pierre hung up and the line went dead. Kate clicked off the phone and set it down. "We've lost them."

"Are you sure?"

She nodded as she caught the hint of anger in his eyes. He'd warned her not to come. Told her to stay in Dallas and let him and the police handle the situation. And she'd done the opposite. *And* potentially almost got them both killed.

"I'm sorry," she started.

"Sorry? This fiasco you just involved us both in could have got us killed."

Marcus drove around the block three times until he was certain they'd lost their tail—and his anger had managed to subside slightly—before heading toward the safe house.

He glanced at her expression out of the corner

of his eye. He could tell she was upset. Her hands were still shaking and her face had paled to a snowy-white color. At least she'd found the courage to do what he'd asked her to, but that didn't excuse the fact that she'd disobeyed his instructions and flown halfway around the world on some mad quest to save her niece. If the police hadn't been able to find the young girl yet with all of their resources, why in the world did she assume she could?

And how had her situation somehow managed to penetrate his normally fortified heart?

He mentally discarded the last question to deal with later. Or not at all. His focus was on closing this case. Period.

"Do you know where we are?" Kate asked.

He fought back a sharp retort. Before she jumped on his navigational skills, she had some explaining to do. "Yes. And I'm taking you to a safe house."

"I checked into a hotel this morning. I'll be fine there."

"If they can find you on the street, don't you think they can find you at your hotel?"

The question silenced her.

He gripped the steering wheel, regretting the tone of his response. He needed time to think, because he didn't have time to take on her responsibility on top of everything else. But now he was going to have to arrange to send her back to the United States and ensure her safety in the meantime.

He kept his gaze straight ahead, watching the maze of cars around him while at the same time glancing frequently into the rearview mirror to ensure they weren't being followed again. "I know you're scared, but I need some answers. Start from the beginning. What in the world are you doing in Paris?"

"I—"

"Because I remember specifically telling you to stay in Dallas with your sister," he continued, not giving her a chance to answer. "And yet somewhere you got the crazy notion that you could take care of things by yourself."

A taxi flew past them, forcing him to swerve into another lane, adding to the tension in his gut. The next time he went out he was going to forget driving, stick to Pierre's advice and use public transportation. Because if whoever was after them didn't get them both killed, driving in Paris certainly could.

Her voice matched his own frustration when she finally answered his question. "What did you expect me to do? Sit in that hospital and wait? The doctors aren't sure Rachel will ever wake up. And no one has found Sophie yet."

"Listen." He worked to soften his voice. "I really do understand that this is hard for you, but it's not your job to go running after a bunch of felons. You're lucky you're not dead, because these guys mean business." He glanced at her again, fighting to hold in his irritation. "You have no idea what you've gotten yourself involved in."

"I didn't choose to get involved in this."

She might be right, but his anger had yet to fully alleviate. "Even so, it didn't mean you should just hop on a plane to track down a man with known criminal ties."

She stared straight ahead out the window at the passing shops, her frown deepening. "It seemed like the right thing to do twenty-four hours ago."

"This isn't a game, Kate. You saw your sister. And you saw what happened just now. These guys play to win."

"Do you think I don't realize that?" She gripped the door handle and turned to him. "They just tried to grab me off the street in broad daylight."

"I saw them grab you. That's why I came after you." Marcus slowed to a stop, waited for the pedestrians to cross, then turned into the underground parking garage and proceeded down the narrow entrance, which explained why all cars in this city were compact.

"Tell me what I should do now." Her voice shook, despite the determination in her voice.

He squeezed into an empty parking space, then shut off the motor, his mind still running through his options regarding what he was going to do with her. His first choice was to send her back to Dallas on the next flight.

"We've got a safe house set up. You can stay there until I can get you a flight back to the States."

"I'm not going back."

He frowned, but he hadn't expected an easy fight. "You don't have a choice, and besides, you'll be safe—"

"Safe?" She unbuckled her seat belt and turned to him, the panic in her voice back. "I'm not sure there is anywhere safe. They found Rachel. And now, for some reason, they think I'm involved and found me here. And the crazy thing is that I don't even know who I'm running from. But I do have a choice as to whether I stay or not."

"I told you not to get involved, and from what I've seen this morning, I was right."

"And you think I'll be safer in Dallas? My sister wasn't safe."

"Listen, Kate. I know you're scared." He pulled out the keys from the ignition and clutched them between his fingers. Arguing wasn't going to get them anywhere for the moment. He needed to change the subject. "Can you think of any reason why they would come after you?"

Marcus's phone rang again. He picked it up. Pierre.

"Give me a second," he told her. "I'll walk you up to the apartment."

He stepped out of the car. "Hey. What have you got?"

"The car you asked me to look up was stolen."

"Figures."

"And the girl?"

"She's with me. Safe for the moment."

"What are you going to do with her?"

"My plan is to ship her out on the next flight back to the United States. I don't have time to babysit."

"Not so fast. We might need her."

Marcus leaned against the car and shook his head. "Why? She's just arrived in the country and brought me nothing but trouble."

"My point exactly. Why are they after her? Neither of us believe in coincidences, so she has to be connected to the case somehow."

Marcus tapped his fingers on the side of the car, unconvinced. He'd meant it when he'd told her she should leave things up to the authorities. He started pacing the small space between his car and the next. "I don't know."

"You know I'm right. Bring her to the safe house, and let her stay there. You can try to find out what she knows. Use her as a bridge to find Chad."

"I'm not going to assume responsibility for her."

"What's wrong with playing the hero who saves the damsel in distress, as you Americans seem to love so much? We need a break in the case, and she might be exactly what we're looking for."

Marcus rubbed the back of his neck with his free hand, ignoring the hero-damsel comparison. According to Kate, she didn't need a hero to sweep in and save her. Which was fine with him. But maybe Pierre did have a point. If she stayed in Paris, he might be able to get some information out of her *and* keep his eye on her at the same time. For as much as he didn't like the idea, as far as he was concerned, Kate Elliot needed someone to look after her.

Kate watched Marcus pace outside the car, cell phone pressed against his ear, his frown deepening. She knew he was talking about her. More than likely, he was having his friend book the next flight out of the country for her. But if Sophie was here, she was going to do everything in her power to help find her niece. And there was nothing Marcus could do to stop her.

When he finally slipped back into the car, she was ready to argue her case. "I'm not leaving Paris."

"That's fine."

"That's fine?" Kate paused. "You're not taking me to the airport?"

"That was my first choice, but Pierre convinced me that we might be able to use you."

"I don't understand."

"Whoever tried to grab you today clearly thinks you are connected to the case somehow. I want to know how. And in exchange, you get a safe place to stay."

Five minutes later, Kate stepped out of the small elevator onto the fourth floor of the apartment building, into a lit hallway with three doors, still unsure if she was happy with the situation. But if it kept her safe and in Paris, maybe it was time to stop arguing.

Marcus pressed the buzzer of apartment 403, then waited beside her until a man wearing a suit opened up the door and ushered them inside.

"This is Pierre Durand." Marcus introduced the man. "He's with French intelligence, working on the same case I am. He also speaks perfect English."

The older man pushed back his glasses and grinned. "From living in Boston for three years."

Kate shook the man's hand and realized her own was still trembling. She pulled her hand back then glanced around the tiny apartment's living room with its mismatched table and chairs and eclectic collection of artwork on the walls. Even the late-morning sunlight streaming through two large windows wasn't enough to lighten her somber mood.

Her gaze shifted back to the other agent. The reality of why she was here hit afresh like an aftershock. She needed a few minutes alone to get her emotions in check.

"You'll find the apartment small, but sufficient. And safe," Pierre assured her. "It's completely off the grid."

"It's . . . perfect. Would you mind if I used the restroom?"

"Of course not." Pierre nodded. "It's straight ahead through the door on the left."

Once inside the narrow room, Kate sat down on the closed toilet seat and rested her hands against her thighs, trying to stop her legs from shaking. Marcus might be used to going after the bad guys, but she wasn't. Which was why he'd been right. Maybe she should be on the next flight back to the United States. She could still feel the man's steel grip on her arm and hear the cars whizzing past her as she'd fled through the heavy traffic.

If she hadn't escaped the vehicle . . . If Marcus hadn't rescued her . . . No. She shook her head. She couldn't let her mind go there. They might still be after her, but for now she *was* safe—even if she wasn't completely comfortable with her rescuer.

Clearly, she had trust issues, springing from the fact that most men in her life hadn't exactly lived up to her expectations. That group primarily included Kevin, who she'd once seen as her hero.

She clenched her fingers together. The bottom

line was that she was scared. Scared that her by and large orderly world had spun out of control to the point that no one—not even the far-too-handsome Agent O'Brian—would be able to set it right again.

Her phone rang, disrupting her tremulous thoughts.

She answered the call, determined to keep her voice even. "Mom?"

"Kate? You sound like you've been crying."

Kate wiped her cheek then pressed her palm against her thigh. "I'm okay. What time is it there?"

"Around five. I couldn't sleep, and I wanted to make sure you arrived safe."

"I did. I'm . . . I'm fine." She wasn't going to tell her mom what had happened. The last thing she needed was a second daughter to worry about. "What's the latest news on Rachel?"

"I'm at the hospital now." There was a long pause on the line. "There's been no change. And no news on the search for Sophie, either."

"I know, Mom, and I'm sorry. So, so sorry."

"I still can't believe what happened, but for the moment, I'm worried about you. I don't think you should have left."

Kate rubbed the back of her neck, trying to iron out the knots that had formed the past twenty-four hours. She knew her mom was hurting. The last thing she wanted to do was add to her worry.

"You understand that I couldn't just sit around and do nothing, Mom."

"Did you find Chad?"

"No. He's not answering his phone. I think he's avoiding me."

"I always knew he wasn't good for Rachel."

"We don't know that he's behind this—"

"Then why isn't he here with Rachel, or at least out looking for his daughter?"

"I don't know, Mom. But I promise I'll call you if I find out anything. Just don't worry about me. I'm safe. In fact, I'm here right now with the agent I met at Rachel's house. Agent O'Brian. He's promised to help, and to keep me safe. We're going to find a way through this."

Kate hung up the call a minute later and drew in a deep breath. For Rachel's sake—for all of them—she was going to have to pull herself together if she was going to find Sophie.

FOUR

Marcus glanced at his watch, then knocked on the door of the restroom, worried about Kate. “Kate, are you okay?”

She blew her nose. “Yeah, I’ll be out in a minute.”

His mind kept switching back and forth from relief that she was safe to anger over the fact that she clearly had no idea how to follow instructions. She’d almost gotten herself kidnapped. Or worse. Which was why—no matter what Pierre might have convinced him—he still believed she had no business being here in Paris, no business trying to track down a killer on her own and especially no business worming her way into his heart.

Because he knew how that scenario was going to end before it even started.

He drummed his fingers against his legs, irritated he’d allowed the thought to even cross his mind. He’d learned a hard lesson with Nicole. She’d become the perfect example of how mixing romance and a high-stress job was nothing more than a recipe for failure. He’d once believed—even if it had been briefly—that she was the one. Beautiful in an exotic way, she’d managed to turn his world upside-down in the few months they'd known each other. He'd decided she was worth the risk, but he'd been wrong. Very wrong.

Nicole had forced him to choose between his career and her. He'd tried to convince her there didn't need to be a choice, but she clearly hadn't agreed. She'd told him she was tired of his busy schedule, of him not being there when she needed him and of constantly worrying he'd be shot . . . or worse.

Marcus stared at the closed door. Kate, though, was nothing like Nicole.

He erased that last thought—something he was doing far too often—because the bottom line was that it really didn't matter what she was like. He moved across the room to look out the window onto the quiet street below, lined with apartments, cafés and a small neighborhood grocery store. He'd always loved Paris. There was something about the people, centuries of history and even the endless miles of subways that had intrigued him. He was used to traveling and dealing with the local authorities. What he hadn't expected was the emotional reaction this case had managed to bring with it.

And Kate Elliot was at the root of that unexpected response.

"She's pretty," Pierre said as Marcus stared out the window.

Marcus turned to the Frenchman. "She's a handful."

"I think I'd be enjoying the challenge, if I were you."

"Don't get any ideas."

Pierre's eyes widened. "You seem to be taking this case rather personally."

Marcus swallowed his frustration. "It's personal because I've been working this for a long time. Every time I think we're about to close in on another lead, something goes wrong. At this point, Chad Laurent is our best lead, but now his wife is lying in the hospital, his daughter is missing and we can't find him. Something's wrong."

Pierre nodded at the bathroom door. "Does she know Chad's connection to the diamonds and weapons smuggling?"

He shook his head. "I haven't told her anything about that."

"I still say we use her to get to Chad."

Marcus lowered his voice. "And I still don't want her to be bait."

"She's the man's sister-in-law. Maybe she can help us bring him in, because frankly, we can't afford to let him get away again. She might be the best chance we've got."

"I don't know."

"You know I'm right. Don't let your sense of chivalry get under your skin and taint the situation. Like I told you on the phone, we need her."

Marcus frowned. His negative reaction to Pierre's suggestion had nothing to do with chivalry or shows of gallantry. He was simply doing his job. Nothing more, nothing less. Kate had already managed to get herself into enough trouble on her own. How much more of a mess would she get into if they used her to hunt down Chad?

Two minutes later, Kate stepped into the living room, looking more put together than when he'd first found her on the street. He could tell she'd been crying, but he didn't blame her. She was lucky she was still alive. The guys who'd been after her played for keeps.

And despite his frustration toward her, he had to give her some credit. She was smart, intuitive and clearly took the initiative. Three characteristics he admired. But that admiration of Kate's characteristics was bound to get him into a heap of trouble if he didn't stop now and rein in his meandering thoughts.

"How about I run across the street and get some coffee and sandwiches for the three of us?" Pierre offered. "I don't know about you, but I missed breakfast."

Marcus nodded. "Thanks. That would be nice."

He sat down on the edge of a plaid, padded armchair in the living room, feeling awkward as Pierre left them alone. But it was time to get to work. He had a number of questions to ask, and he needed answers. Not that this was an interrogation, not officially at least, but there were things he wanted to know before they could go any further and he was convinced she knew things that could help him find Chad.

"Why don't you sit down. If it hasn't already, jet lag will be hitting you soon."

She nodded, then sat down on the couch across from him.

He reached into his briefcase, pulled out Rachel's journal and photo albums, and set them on the wooden coffee table between them.

Kate's gaze narrowed as she recognized them. "You read her journal?"

"It's evidence."

"Evidence?" Kate stood up and started pacing in front of him. "Do you know how upset my sister would be knowing the government is reading her private thoughts?"

Marcus tapped the floor with his foot at the fumble he'd clearly just made. This wasn't the way to get her to help him. "I'm sorry, but she doesn't have too much to worry about. So far, I haven't been able to decipher much of it."

"My sister has her own kind of shorthand."

"So I've discovered. I was hoping you would be able to help me interpret it. Do you think you can read it?"

She stopped pacing and caught his gaze. "It's my sister's journal."

"I know, but you want to find your niece." He opened the book to a marked page, then handed it to her. "For example, who's Ace? She mentions him around the time she was in Paris."

"I don't know. Rachel . . . she always makes up nicknames for people."

"Like?"

"Growing up she called me Kit Kat. Sophie's always been Pumpkin."

"And Chad?"

"She called him Beau."

"So this name . . . Ace . . . could be anyone."

"Yes. I'm sorry. I really don't know. Why do you want to find him?"

"I'm the one asking the questions for the moment."

She plopped back onto the couch. "In case you haven't noticed, I'm not the enemy here. I will do anything I can to help my sister and find my niece—including working with you—but I don't know why that needs to include an interrogation."

"I'm sorry." Marcus pinched the bridge of his noise. He needed to quit saying he was sorry, as much as he needed her to understand he was trying to help. "This isn't an interrogation. Listen. I'll make you a deal. Let me ask you what I need to know, then I'll answer anything you want."

"Anything?"

"Anything."

His phone rang, and he grabbed it out of his front pocket. She was right. She didn't deserve to be put in a position where she felt like the enemy.

A moment later he hung up the phone and slipped it back into his pocket. "Our conversation will have to wait. They need me down at the station in regards to that stolen car that chased us."

She scooted forward on the couch. "I'll come with you—"

"I don't think that's a good idea right now, but I'll be back in an hour or so." He tried to ignore the disappointment in her eyes. "Pierre is on his way with lunch, along with one of the female French agents, who will stay here with you until I get back."

"I don't need a babysitter," she shot back.

"If I remember correctly, you were needing a bit of help when I showed up."

Her frown deepened, making him feel guilty again for provoking her.

"Kate, please. I'm not trying to argue with you." He paused while trying to categorize his thoughts. "This isn't personal. I just want to keep you safe."

Except it was becoming personal. No matter how he tried to keep things strictly business, his heart wasn't complying. She stared up at him with those wide eyes, making him want to draw her into his arms and promise her that he'd fix everything. Which irritated him all the more. He'd never had problems keeping his professional life separate from his personal life. Kate Elliot was just another case. A source he might be able to use to his advantage.

Nothing more. Nothing less.

But if that was true, then why did his heart wish he could stay?

Kate's phone rang, jolting her awake. She opened her eyes and stared at the sunlight filtering through flowery drapes, trying to figure out where she was. Her mind clicked through the events of the past forty-eight hours in rapid succession. Rachel'd been shot. Sophie was missing. She was in Paris. And Marcus . . . She still wasn't sure what to think about the too-good-looking agent.

She grabbed the phone off the bedside table of the room she'd been given. Marcus had left the apartment after a call, leaving her with Jocelyn and Pierre, who'd thankfully left her alone for the most part without hounding her with too many more questions. After lunch, Jocelyn, the forty-something-year-old agent with ebony skin and dark brown eyes, had suggested Kate take a short nap until Marcus returned in order to fight off the jet lag, and Kate had agreed.

She checked the caller ID.

Chad?

Kate's stomach lurched as she quickly sat up and answered the phone. "Chad? Where are you?"

"You shouldn't have gotten involved," he said.

She glanced at the closed door of her bedroom and lowered her voice. "I shouldn't have gotten involved? Rachel was shot, and you're telling me that I shouldn't have gotten involved?"

"I'm sorry." There was a long pause on the line. "All of this is my fault."

"Why?"

"I can't tell you."

"Then at least tell me where you are. We need to talk."

"We can't meet."

"I'm not here to play games, Chad. You owe me an explanation."

"Who's the man you were with this morning?"

He knew about Marcus?

"What man?" she asked.

"You got into a car with him."

"He's just a friend. Someone I met back in the States recently." She might not be sure what to think about the good-looking agent, but that didn't mean Chad needed to know she was helping the FBI. Not yet, anyway. "How do you know?"

"That doesn't matter, but don't lie to me, Kate. He's with the authorities."

She hesitated briefly. "They want to make sure

I'm safe. Your friends . . . or whoever they were . . . tried to grab me off the street."

"I'm sorry about that, but I can't have the police involved."

"You keep saying you're sorry." Kate heard her voice rise a notch. "But sorry doesn't exactly cut it. Just tell me where Sophie is, and I'll be happy to leave. With her."

"I don't know. You have to believe me. I never meant for any of this to happen. They . . ." His voice trailed off.

"They what, Chad?"

"I can't tell you. I'm in far too deep."

Kate frowned, but she wasn't about to give up. She needed a different approach. "I have a feeling we can help each other. Please."

Another long pause followed. Kate's heart pounded. She had to make this work.

"Chad?"

"I'll talk to you, if you come alone. You'll have to make sure you aren't followed."

"I'll do anything you say, if it helps find Sophie."

"Can you get to Notre Dame by two o'clock?"

Kate glanced at the clock on the bedside table. That would give her an hour. The safe house was in the Latin Quarter, and while she wasn't sure how far it was, walking should be an option. "I'll be there."

"But, Kate . . . if I find out that you have a tail,

I'll disappear and I promise, you'll never see me again."

Marcus walked down the crowded street in the heart of the Latin Quarter from the metro and was reminded as to why he loved this city. The safe house they'd secured was located in an eighteenth-century building, a perfect place to disappear. Winding cobblestone streets were filled with quaint cafés, restaurants, boutiques and open markets, along with famous museums and squares. To anyone who saw him walking toward the historic apartment building, he was just another happy tourist here on holiday.

"Marcus?" Pierre's voice came through his radio earpiece, reminding him he wasn't here to relax. The lead he'd gone in for had been nothing more than another dead end. It was time they finished this.

Marcus pushed on the earpiece. "Go ahead, Pierre."

"I've got good news and bad news."

"Something tells me I'm not going to like this."

Marcus stopped in front of a pasta restaurant with a wide red awning and tables, filled with customers, set up along the sidewalk. "What's going on?"

"Kate received a phone call, then slipped out of the apartment—"

"She what?"

"Jocelyn and I were in the kitchen talking. We thought she was still in her room on the phone."

"You've got to be kidding me." Marcus started walking again, quickening his pace down the street toward the apartment. "What in the world was she thinking?"

"We're thinking one of two things. Either Chad called or the kidnappers called."

Marcus agreed. More than likely, neither of them would want the authorities involved. And as for Kate, his clear, simple instructions to stay put the next hour hadn't been enough.

"How long ago?"

"Five . . . ten minutes at the most. She's not answering her phone, but she's headed in the direction of Notre Dame."

"How do you know?"

"That's the good news. We just managed to catch up with her." Pierre gave him their location. "She's a block ahead of us."

"Then you need to catch up with her and bring her in."

"I'm not sure that's the best idea," Pierre began.

Marcus frowned. "What do you mean?"

As far as he was concerned, the *best* idea would have been to go with his gut instincts and already have her on the next flight to the United States. She clearly didn't trust him, which was going to make it difficult to get her to help them.

"I say we keep following her without her knowing we're onto her and see who she's going to meet. Because if we step in now, we could very easily blow a potentially huge lead."

"No way." Marcus paused at the intersection with a group of pedestrians waiting for the light to change. "This morning these goons tried to grab her off the street, which means they know she's here. If we let her go without any kind of plan in place, we can't make any guarantees about her safety."

Once again, he had to give her credit for the fact that she was gutsy, and would clearly do anything to find her niece. But if it was the kidnappers she was planning to meet, they were looking at an entirely different scenario. Pulling her out now seemed like the wisest decision, because either way, he wasn't willing to put Kate's life at risk again.

He felt another line of defense crack within him. Why was it that those very strengths she was demonstrating right now were managing to make it so hard for him to separate personal from business? Because whether or not he wanted to admit it, she *was* managing to find a way through that fortified heart of his.

"And if your plan doesn't work?" Marcus finally asked. "It's too dangerous. She's emotional, tired and running on adrenaline. Add jet lag to the mix and we're simply asking for trouble."

"Dangerous?" Pierre asked.

"What if we lose her?"

Half a dozen scenarios flashed through his mind, including her being snatched up by a bunch of thugs who sold illegal weapons for a living.

"I don't know about the qualifications of your FBI, but we were trained for situations like this."

"You're the one who lost her in the first place." The light turned and Marcus hurried across the street.

"Funny. Risks are a reality in any situation, Marcus. You can't tie the girl to a chair and expect her to sit still."

"Maybe, but I don't think we should risk her life unnecessarily—"

"And if someone is watching her, contacting her now could actually put her life at risk. If she calls and tells you her plans, great. But until then, we're going to follow at a distance until we find out who she's meeting."

FIVE

Three blocks later, Marcus found Kate. He followed her from a distance down the narrow Parisian street, past a line of cafés and bakeries topped with sky-high apartments. He stayed far enough back so she wouldn't realize he was behind her. Close enough he wouldn't lose her. Pierre walked a few steps ahead of him on the opposite side of the street smoking a cigarette, while Jocelyn kept a closer guard. Further backup was in place if Kate decided to jump into a cab.

Pierre had assured him that their plan was virtually foolproof, but it was the word *virtually* that had him worried. There were no guarantees in a situation like this. The only way he could guarantee her safety was if they would have escorted her back to the apartment—which he should have insisted on. A decision he regretted not making. Except Pierre had been right about one thing. Acting with his heart and not his head was bound to get him into a heap of trouble.

But true or not, toying with Kate's life left him uneasy. If everything went according to the plan, they could end up with Chad in custody, which would allow him to send Kate on the next flight back to the United States. If things didn't go as planned, they could have a disaster on their hands.

Kate slipped around the corner, into a busy outdoor market.

"Do you see her?" Pierre asked, picking up his pace on the other side of the street.

"No . . ." Marcus searched the crowd for her short, red print dress. "She melted into the crowd when she turned around the corner."

"I don't see her now, either," Jocelyn said. "What was the description she gave of the men who grabbed her?"

Marcus's regret over his decision to go along with Pierre's plan mounted. "One was . . . balding . . . fortyish with tattoo sleeves on his forearms. The other one was short and stocky. Red curly hair. We can't lose her."

Marcus turned the corner. Vendors called out to get his attention. Marcus forced down the panic as he picked up his pace, searching for Kate past vendors selling fresh fruits, vegetables and buckets of flowers.

"Do you see her yet?" he repeated.

"No," Pierre and Jocelyn said in unison over the radio.

Marcus wove his way through the crowd past books, paintings and other bric-a-brac. The way his luck was running, Pierre's risky idea was about to blow up in their face. Kate might not have made the smartest move, but he hadn't done anything to stop her.

Which meant if anything happened to her it would be his fault.

He knew these people. They played for keeps. They would find her, get what they wanted from her, then kill her.

Marcus sidestepped a pair of shoppers, their bags loaded with fresh vegetables. "Jocelyn . . . do you see her?"

"Wait a minute."

"Tell me what you see, Jocelyn."

"It wasn't her, but I think I see a bald man that might be who we're looking for . . . He's twenty meters ahead of me, walking in the direction she was headed."

Marcus clenched his fists beside him. How in the world had all three of them managed to lose her? And they still weren't certain where she was going. The meeting place could be anything from Notre Dame, to a local café, to one of the bridges. What was she doing?

Marcus stopped in the middle of the market and weighed his options. He'd tried doing things Pierre's way. This time he was going to do things his way.

"I'm going to call her," he said.

"If she had agreed to meet with him—without the authorities—you could blow everything, and possibly get her killed."

"I'm calling her."

He punched in the number he had programmed

on speed dial in case he needed to contact her. He let the phone ring a dozen times. No answer. He hung up and punched Redial.

Pick up, Kate. Come on . . .

What if they missed her going into one of the cafés or shops? He glanced into the nearest shop, looking for a sign of her red dress, and let the phone ring. Still no answer.

Where are you, Kate?

The girl was playing with fire and had no idea what the men she was up against were capable of doing.

Kate breathed in the aroma of freshly baked bread as she hurried through the crowded market, certain she was being followed. Last year, poachers had targeted her close friend while they were working on a wildlife documentary in South Africa. Kate had seen the fallout from people's evil choices, and it wasn't anything like what one saw on TV. It was real and people got hurt.

Which was why she was regretting her decision to slip out of the apartment without telling Marcus what she was planning to do. She should have called him and told him the truth. Told him that Chad had called and agreed to meet her. Chad might have insisted she come alone, but she never should have agreed to his demands. If nothing else, she could have asked Marcus to meet her at the church without Chad knowing.

He was an FBI agent. He had to know how to shadow someone covertly. Just knowing he was there would have upped her confidence immeasurably. But now it was too late. She was certain she'd spotted the bald man who'd tried to grab her earlier following her in the crowd. They'd tried once to grab her off the streets in broad daylight. What made her think that they might not try again?

Kate stopped in front of a display of colorful Parisian scarves, and glanced into the mirror hanging up for customers so she could see the crowded street behind her. Women carrying baskets shopped for fresh produce. Tourists bartered for trinkets.

She turned around, then plunged back into the crowd. *Someone* was following her. She was certain of it. Her chest heaved, lungs screaming for air as she pushed through the crowd, past dozens of stalls, their colors blurring together. She could hear people shouting in French while music played in the background. She needed to go somewhere safe.

Please, God . . . I don't know where to go.

Kate's phone vibrated, breaking into her thoughts. She shoved her hand into her pocket and pulled out her phone. She hesitated.

Caller unknown.

It could be Chad changing the meeting place,

or her mother with an update on Rachel. Or it could be Sophie's kidnappers.

The phone buzzed again, and she answered the call. "Hello?"

"Kate. It's Marcus."

Marcus? Kate let out a sharp breath of relief, ignoring the twinge of guilt that surfaced. She never should have left the apartment alone, but she'd only been thinking about Sophie. And finding Sophie had to be her first priority.

"Marcus, I . . ."

"Are you okay?"

Kate kept walking through the crowd, weaving in and out of stalls hoping to lose whoever was behind her. "I'm not sure. I think I'm being followed."

"Where are you? We know you left the apartment."

We?

Kate stopped in front of a display of pink roses and turned around. Marcus was clearly looking for her, as well.

She let out a sharp exhale. If he was here as well . . . "I figured it wouldn't take you too long to notice I was gone. I just thought . . ."

"You thought if you didn't tell me, I wouldn't try to follow?" he asked. "The thing is, Kate, we're on the same side. You should have told me you needed to leave. I would have provided protection."

"I'm sorry, but I didn't think I could take that chance. Chad told me to come alone, but now . . . but now I think they've found me. I can feel it."

She studied the crowd. There was no sign of the bald man . . . or Marcus. Maybe she really had lost him.

"Tell me where you are, Kate."

She glanced around for a point of reference. "I don't know. In the market. There are flowers everywhere."

She slipped into the shadows between two of the flower stalls, where she could watch everyone who walked by, debating what she should do. "Chad called me. Told me he'd only talk to me if I came alone."

"Let me help you, Kate. Give me a street name . . . a corner . . . anything and I'll come to you."

She glanced at the end of the market, where cars were passing by. "I can't. Chad said no cops. If he has her, I can't take any chances of putting Sophie's life further at risk."

"You can, because you're in way over your head. And because I can help. I promise, Kate. It's going to be okay."

She hesitated, then gave him the street address where she was, praying she was making the right decision.

"There's a café a block to your right with a few tables inside," Marcus said. "Meet me there."

• • •

Marcus stopped along the sidewalk next to a stand displaying fresh fish. Pierre and Jocelyn were still looking for her while he kept talking. She might not have agreed to let him help her yet, but at least she hadn't hung up.

"I need you to trust me, Kate." Marcus tried to put himself in her place while waiting for her answer. She was scared, vulnerable, trying to save her family halfway around the world . . . No wonder the girl was confused.

"I know the guys Chad is involved with," he continued, thankful she still hadn't hung up. "I've been after them for over twelve months. They won't hesitate to kill anyone who gets in the way. And after this morning, they know you're here, and apparently think you have something they need. Which means, like it or not, we need each other, Kate."

"Who are they?"

"Meet me at the café, and I'll tell you what I know. Trust me, Kate."

He pressed his phone against his ear, not wanting to miss her response because of the noise of the crowd.

"Okay, but I'm not making any promises. I can't miss Chad. He's expecting me, and this might be my only chance."

Marcus glanced at his watch. "Where are you meeting him?"

She hesitated again. “In front of Notre Dame at two.”

“I can ensure you get there in time without him knowing you’ve got protection.”

He could tell her resolve was wavering.

“I’ll be there,” she said then hung up.

Pierre spoke into his microphone a moment later. “You shouldn’t have called her.”

“Maybe not, but you know as well as I do that we can’t lose this opportunity. We also have to protect her.”

Marcus slipped his phone into his pocket. He caught sight of her red dress in front of the café as she slipped inside. How in the world had she managed to lose three trained agents?

Two minutes later, he slid into the chair across from her. “You shouldn’t have left the apartment without telling me,” he said.

“I didn’t think I had a choice. Which is why I’ll give you ten minutes to convince me you can help me, but then I’m leaving. Like I told you, I can’t take any chance at missing Chad. Of losing a chance to find Sophie.”

The waitress came by and he ordered two coffees for them in French.

“Are you hungry?” he asked.

“A little. My stomach isn’t sure what time it is.”

“Sweet or savory?”

Kate glanced at the glass case filled with dozens of pastries. “Sweet, I guess.”

He spoke to the woman again, ordering something he hoped she'd like.

"What did you order?"

He shot her a smile and watched her shoulders relax slightly, along with her jaw. "A surprise. You'll like it."

Trust me.

He wanted her to trust him. To let him help her. To believe she didn't have to tackle this on her own.

"I didn't know you were so fluent in French," she said as soon as the waitress left.

He couldn't decide if she was impressed or just trying to ease the awkwardness between them.

"Enough to get me a good cup of coffee, one of those to-die-for pastries and a few other basic things."

"You're too modest. And you shouldn't have come after me."

"I was trying to keep you safe. When I lost you . . ." He wasn't going to tell her yet just how worried he'd been. How he'd never have forgiven himself if something had happened to her.

He swallowed hard. "Let's just say that this isn't a game, Kate, and I don't want anything to happen to you."

Kate nodded and folded her hands in front of her on the table. "I don't mean to sound like I don't appreciate what you've done. Really. I showed up halfway around the world determined to find my niece, and all you've done so far is come to my rescue."

"It's my job."

She nodded. "I know."

Only that wasn't entirely true. Because for some crazy reason, Kate didn't seem like just a job anymore. He could continue trying to convince himself that this was just another case. That *she* was just another piece of a puzzle, but it had somehow become more than that.

"I need you to understand," she continued, "that as much as I appreciate what you've done, I have to find my niece. And if that means meeting my brother-in-law in the middle of the afternoon in front of Notre Dame, alone, then I have to take that risk."

"But that's the point." He leaned forward and caught her gaze. "You don't have to. You don't have to do this on your own."

He sat back, momentarily distracted as the waitress set down two cups of coffee and pastries in front of them.

Kate's eyes widened. "Wow."

Hers was topped with strawberries, blackberries and raspberries.

"Inside that crisp, round exterior is gooey vanilla," he said. "You're going to love it."

She dug her fork into the middle and tasted the dessert. "Who are they? The men after me."

"They're involved in smuggling diamonds into

the US from Africa, primarily, in exchange for military-grade weapons for various terrorist groups."

Her eyes widened. "Diamonds and weapons . . . and you think Chad is involved."

"He's definitely connected, which is why I'm looking for him. And why I want you to let me help. You can do it on your own and risk not only Sophie's life, but your own, or you can let me help you. I have a backup team, tech support, everything we need to guarantee things go our way."

"You can't make those kinds of guarantees. If you're so good, why haven't you already taken down these guys?"

He ignored the barb. Because she was right. "We're going to find them, because I have no plans on stopping until they're behind bars. They've hurt a lot of innocent people, and I don't want you to be one of them."

"But you're still willing to use me to catch them. Isn't that why you were following me?"

"Would you have said yes, if I'd asked to come with you?" he asked. The girl didn't miss much. "Pierre thought we could—"

"Use me as bait." She dumped the packet of sugar into her coffee and stirred it slowly. "I figured that one out."

"I wouldn't use the word *bait*. We were worried you wouldn't let us go with you."

"You're right. I wouldn't have. Because I need to see Chad, and he won't talk to me if I'm surrounded by bodyguards and FBI agents. He made that very clear."

"He's probably just scared, Kate. So do it my way. You talk to him, and we ensure nothing goes wrong. We saw the guy who tried to grab you earlier this morning. He was in the market. You need the extra protection."

"But then what happens to Chad? You arrest him?"

"Right now, all I want to do is bring him in for questioning. Find out what he knows. Then I want to take down the men he's working with and find Sophie, but getting yourself kidnapped or killed in the process certainly isn't going to help." He watched her expression as she sipped her coffee and ate her pastry. "Why'd you answer?"

"Honestly?" Her eyes softened. "Because I'm scared, and confused, and want to put an end to this, but I don't know how."

Marcus took a bite of his caramelized apple pastry. "Then maybe we're on the same page after all."

Kate studied the man sitting across from her. His expression was focused, determined. She had no doubt that he was good at what he did, or that she could trust him. Which she did. But today had made her head spin. Left her feeling as though she were drowning, and she couldn't come up for air.

He was throwing her a life buoy. She needed to grab hold of it.

"Chad won't talk to me if I'm followed," she said, taking her last bite of the pastry that had her wishing for seconds.

She glanced out the window at the bustling street with its open-air markets, whimsical boutiques and boulangeries. Sitting here drinking coffee in a French café, the City of Love . . . the City of Lights . . . La Ville-Lumière . . .

Visiting this city had always been a dream. Chasing down the person who had kidnapped her niece had never been a part of the plan. One day she was going to return to Paris with someone who could show her the city.

Like Marcus.

Kate swallowed the last few sips of her coffee, trying to choke down the ridiculous thought. She'd panicked today, and Marcus had come through for her like some gallant hero. But that wasn't a reason to let her mind run wild with romantic thoughts that included him as her champion.

"We'll arrive separately," he was saying. "I'll make sure Chad doesn't know you're being followed."

Kate forced herself to focus. "What if you lose me, or if he discovers that FBI is there?"

"I'll make sure that doesn't happen." Marcus set his empty coffee cup and saucer on top of his pastry dish and shoved them both forward. "Kate, we need Chad and right now you're my only link to him. I need your help. And you need my protection."

"I have to ask for one more thing before I say yes."

"Name it."

"Can you ensure my sister and mother's safety?"

"I'll talk to my boss and have a team sent in to ensure they're safe. And I promise I will do everything in my power not only to protect you and your family, but to ensure your niece is found."

I need You to help protect them as well, God. There are so many things that seem completely out of my control.

"I don't know about your faith," he continued, "but I also plan to do a lot of praying."

She looked up and caught Marcus's gaze. "Me, too."

The butterflies had yet to settle in her stomach, but at least she wasn't going into this alone.

He reached out and grasped her hands. "We can do this."

"Okay." She nodded. "Let's go."

SIX

Kate walked across the brick pavement toward the majestic Notre Dame looming in front of her. Many believed the famous cathedral to be one of the finest examples of French Gothic architecture in the world, with its flying buttresses, stained glass windows and spiral staircases leading to spectacular views of the city.

But she wasn't here as a tourist. Instead, she searched for Chad among the crowd bustling around her. A couple fed the birds gathered in the square. Uniformed police patrolled the street corners. She glanced at her watch. She was still five minutes early. Chad had always been prompt. If he didn't show, they'd be back to square one.

As he'd promised, there was no sign of Marcus, only the influx of those coming and going from the church. She had to admit that knowing he was in the background helped tame the butterflies chasing each other around in her stomach. Despite her hesitations, she was grateful she'd agreed to listen to his advice.

Tourists with their backpacks and cameras gathered outside the church, where a street musician sang Leonard Cohen's "Hallelujah." She closed her eyes for a moment to listen to the words and let the music settle her nerves. But all she could think about was that her sister was dying and she might not ever see her niece again if she didn't figure out what was going on.

Feeling out of place, she pulled out her cell phone and snapped a photo of the church, trying to remember what else she'd read about the cathedral. It had been constructed with over five thousand gargoyles, held priceless paintings, and the largest bell in the tower was close to four hundred years old and weighed over 28,000 pounds.

She snapped another photo of the front of the building. Rachel had the same shot of the church with her and Sophie standing in front of it from one of their visits to Paris. Smiles on both their faces . . .

"Kate?"

She turned toward the voice. "Chad."

He walked up to her, gray slacks, white button-down shirt and pullover sweater. Kate could see why Rachel had fallen for him with his ruddy good looks and European accent. He'd always been sure of himself, charming enough to sweep Rachel off her feet. Today, he stood beside her, his gaze sweeping the crowd, nervous and clearly leery that someone was watching them.

He shoved his hands into his pockets, stopping beside her as he stared up at the church from the open plaza.

"Stunning, isn't it?"

"Much more so than I expected," she answered.

"Walk with me inside. Visiting the cathedral is free."

She hesitated briefly, then followed Chad through the entrance. While the outside of the building had left her amazed, the inside of the church, with its long halls, vaulted ceilings and the beauty of the soft lighting from stained glass windows, was enough to leave her breathless. But today, even that wasn't enough to shift her focus. She was here for one reason and one reason only.

Chad stopped in front of a votive rack and lit one of the candles. "It might be the most visited cathedral in the world, but I've always found it peaceful here. My mother used to bring me to mass on Sundays, though I suppose today, my going to confession might be more appropriate."

Kate pressed her lips together at the comment. A confession wasn't going to be enough to change what had happened.

He turned away and guided her down the majestic hall, his voice barely above a whisper this time. "Were you followed here?"

"I'm not sure, but I am certain that they know I'm in Paris. I told you two men tried to grab me off the streets already."

"I'm sorry." He kept moving, avoiding her gaze. Clearly scared.

"I'm sorry, too," she said. "I need to know what is going on."

Despite the sense of awe and serenity from walking through the cathedral, anger had settled into the pit of her stomach. In her sister's eyes, Chad had always been the knight who'd rode in and swept Rachel off her feet. How that romantic scenario had turned into her fighting for her life, she had no idea. But it had.

"Tell me what's going on, Chad. How do they know I'm here?" she asked.

"I don't know."

She shook her head, not believing him. He clearly knew much more than he was willing to tell her.

"Then at least tell me who *they* are."

He slipped into one of the rows of pews and sat down, waiting for her to join him. A woman in her mid-forties wearing a pale gray scarf around her neck slipped into a pew behind them, her head bowed in prayer. Across the aisle a mother with her daughter, no more than six, sat down across from them. A coin dropped from the little girl's fingers and rolled under the pew. Kate hesitated as the little girl tugged on her mom's sleeve to help her find the money and started crying.

The image of the girl opened a flood of emotions.

Was Sophie crying right now? Had they hurt her?

She finally took a seat beside him, feeling as if they were two people on a spiritual pilgrimage, trying to figure out who had tried to murder her sister. No one should be trying to discover the truth behind such a horror.

"You don't need to know who they are, or get involved in this," he began.

Kate leaned forward. "Are you kidding me? I'm already involved. In case you've already forgotten—"

He held a finger to his mouth.

She pressed her lips together, then lowered her voice. "They know who I am, and that I'm here in Paris. Tell me why."

She'd only been able to come to one conclusion. Chad was clearly involved in something very serious and very illegal. Beyond that, she was certain they'd been watching her family. For leverage against Chad, perhaps they'd come after Rachel and Sophie. And if Marcus was right, these people had both connections and money. As for her involvement? Maybe they thought she was Rachel? Maybe they thought she knew more than she did, but the bottom line was that Chad was clearly involved in something that had just ripped his family apart. Which was why she had to trust Marcus . . . and find out the truth from Chad.

Chad folded his hands inside his lap and dropped his head. "Rachel . . . how bad is she?"

Kate felt a wave of anger seep through her at Chad's question. As far as she was concerned, what had happened to her sister was Chad's fault.

Whatever he was involved in had trickled down and affected his family.

"I'm surprised you asked."

"We might not have the greatest marriage, but I certainly don't hate her. Besides, she gave me the best thing that ever happened to me. Sophie."

"If you really cared about Sophie, it seems to me that you wouldn't have allowed this to happen in the first place."

"Just tell me she's going to be okay," he said. "Please."

"The bullet missed any major arteries, but it's still serious. She's in ICU and unconscious. I'm waiting for another update from my mother." She hoped her mother had gone home to get some needed sleep, but knowing her mother, she was still at the hospital.

Which was why at the moment there was really only one question that really mattered.

"Where's Sophie, Chad?" she asked.

"I don't know."

"You're telling me that you had nothing to do with Rachel's shooting and Sophie's disappearance."

"Of course not."

"Then who did? Someone used Sophie's passport to bring her here. Who else would do that?"

He turned to her and shook his head. "I swear, I didn't take her, Kate. You have to believe me."

Kate pressed her fingers against the edge of the hard wood bench they sat on. Until talking to Marcus, it had been easy to believe that Chad had been behind Sophie's disappearance. An unhappy father wanting custody of his daughter and deciding to take things into his own hands. Foolish, but common. And for her, a far easier scenario to swallow than believing terrorists were behind Sophie's kidnapping. That was still something she wasn't ready to accept.

"You're telling me you're not behind this?" she pressed.

He reached out and grasped her arm. "You think I took Sophie to get back at Rachel?"

Kate pulled away from his grip. "I don't know what to think at this point."

"You have to believe me. I didn't have anything to do with it."

"Then what do you know? Because the way I'm looking at things, because of you, my sister might not make it another twenty-four hours, Sophie is missing and apparently they're after me as well, because someone thinks I know something, but I don't know anything. I need to know the truth, Chad."

He paused as a couple walked by, snapping photos of the stained glass windows. "I got involved with the wrong people, Kate."

"You got involved with the wrong people. That's your excuse?"

"You have to believe me when I say that it wasn't supposed to happen this way."

"Forget the excuses, just tell me the truth, Chad."

"The truth is that I'm the one they want. They took Sophie to get to me."

"Who are they?" Marcus might have told her that they were middlemen working for the highest bidder, but she wanted to hear the truth from Chad.

"I think they work for my boss, and they believe I've been stealing diamonds from the company I work for."

"And have you?"

Chad's gaze shifted to the floor.

"Chad? Have you been stealing diamonds?"

"Yes."

Kate let out a sharp breath. "How many?"

"Five million dollars' worth over the past two years."

"Five million dollars?" Kate glanced behind them. A group of Japanese tourists had entered the cathedral, but none of them seemed to be paying any attention to them. Tourists continued snapping photos. Studying the intricate panels of stained glass. Staring up at the vaulted ceiling. No one knew or even cared what they were talking about. "You can't be serious. How did you steal them?"

"I smuggled them inside the music boxes I

sent to Sophie for her birthday and Christmas. I planned to return and get them eventually, but I wasn't in a hurry to sell them. It seemed smarter to lay low. Seemed like a perfect hiding place where no one would ever find them, including Rachel."

A perfect hiding place? Instead, he'd foolishly risked both Rachel's and his daughter's lives with his greed.

"And no one noticed they were missing until now?"

"Half of what my company receives is under the table. No paperwork means no paper trail. I've managed to cultivate relationships with some suppliers who are happy to let me get rid of their dirty diamonds. We, on the other hand, pay a fraction of the price."

"Which means more profit for your company, until you decided to keep a portion for yourself."

Which was exactly what Marcus had mentioned to her at the café. Kate tried to sort through the information she had so far. She'd spent time in Africa and had learned enough about blood diamonds to know that the illegally traded stones funded weapons and wars primarily in central and western Africa. Thousands—including children—were used in forced labor to mine the diamonds. And while efforts had been made to stop the trade and ensure that the gems weren't funding the violence of war, clearly there were those who had found a way around it.

And she wanted some answers.

"How did you do it?"

"The diamonds are laundered into the global supply by export houses like ours, then cut and sold on the regular market." There was little expression in Chad's voice. "I skimmed a percentage of those off the top."

Kate stared at the blues and purples of one of the stained glass windows. Rachel had shown her the cylinder music boxes Chad had collected for Sophie, with their melodic sound and Swiss precision. She'd taken one of them to a dealer and discovered they were crafted with burr elm veneers and hand-cut designs. And that they were worth at least two thousand dollars each. Knowing what else had been inside the music boxes, Kate realized the value of those boxes had just skyrocketed.

But when Rachel's relationship with Chad soured after he moved permanently to Paris, she'd packed up the boxes and returned them. Kate had assumed she'd sent them back to Chad. And when Kate had asked why, her sister had told her she wanted a husband who was there for her and Sophie, not one who only knew how to buy his daughter's love.

"But you have the music boxes, Chad."

His eyes widened. "What do you mean?"

Kate shivered, wishing for the warmth of outside. "Rachel returned the music boxes to you. All of them. Or at least I thought she did. She told me she didn't want them. That you were trying to buy Sophie's love."

Chad shook his head. "No . . . no, she didn't return them."

"You're telling me you don't know where the music boxes . . . the diamonds are?"

Chad ran his fingers through his hair and clasped his hands behind his head. "I don't have them, Kate. She never sent them to me."

"Then where are they?"

"I don't know."

Kate gauged his expression and frowned. Something else was wrong. "What did you do, Chad?"

Chad's gaze dropped, his voice still barely above a whisper. "I had someone break into Rachel's house to get the music boxes. You have to understand, they were threatening to kill me if I didn't produce them."

"And when they went to get the music boxes for you, they . . . they shot her instead?"

Kate shook her head. It didn't make sense.

"No . . . they just searched the house for the music boxes while she was out with Sophie, then left empty-handed. Whoever shot her . . . it had to have been someone else. Someone who was there when she returned."

"Someone who decided to use your wife and daughter as leverage to get the diamonds."

Chad nodded.

"Then where are the diamonds?" Kate continued.

"I don't know." Chad raked his hands through his hair again. Drops of perspiration marked his forehead.

"So when they demand the diamonds in exchange for Sophie, you won't have them."

"I was hoping you knew where they were." Chad's hands shook in his lap as he scanned the area around them. "I might have something else I can give them as leverage, but I'm not sure it will be enough. I was planning to turn it in to the police."

"What is it?"

"I . . . I have a list of contacts and a ledger of my company's illegal activities. I've been collecting it as a . . . safety net."

"While you played Russian roulette with your wife's and daughter's lives."

He looked up and caught her gaze. "It wasn't supposed to end up this way."

"Of course it wasn't supposed to end with your daughter being kidnapped and your wife in the hospital, but you decided to get greedy."

"I'm sorry, Kate."

"Sorry doesn't fix anything at this point."

Kate shook her head and tried to focus on the solemn music playing in the background. The place where they sat was more than just a tourist spot. To many, it was a house of worship. A place filled with God's presence. A place of forgiveness. She'd always been taught to forgive, but this . . . this was different. How could she forgive Chad for what he'd done?

"Have you heard from the kidnappers?" she asked finally, breaking the silence between them.

Chad studied a group of tourists walking by. "They called me this morning. They are demanding the diamonds in exchange for Sophie."

"When?"

"On the second level of the Eiffel Tower at nine o'clock tomorrow morning."

Kate felt her stomach turn. No diamonds meant they couldn't meet the demands for Sophie's exchange. There had to be a way out of this. "You have to go to the police and tell them what you know."

"I can't." Chad shook his head. "I have to find the diamonds myself."

"How? If you don't have them . . . and Rachel doesn't have them—"

"I think we should go." Chad started to stand. "If they find us here together . . ."

Kate hesitated as she glanced toward the entrance of the church. Marcus was here somewhere, along with Jocelyn and Pierre. She grabbed his arm. "Wait a minute. I've got someone who can help you."

He sat back down and leaned toward her. "You promised you'd come alone, Kate."

"His name's Marcus O'Brian. He's with the FBI, working with French intelligence."

Chad shook his head. "The authorities will arrest me if they find me. The only reason I decided to talk to you is because I need to find those diamonds."

"Chad, please." Kate tried to curb the desperation in her voice. "Forget about the diamonds and think about Sophie. They can help us get her back. They just want to talk to you. They're after the men who took Sophie. You said you had evidence. They'll listen to you. Make some kind of deal."

Chad drummed his fingers against the pew. "They're here, Kate. And they'll kill me if they find out I can't find the diamonds."

"Who?"

Kate studied the people filing by, looking for the men who'd grabbed her. An older couple. Some American tourists. A group of students with a guide. She glanced back at Chad. Surely he was simply jumping at shadows.

"They're here to make sure I do what they told me to do," he said.

"Where are they, Chad?"

"I was foolish to think I could outsmart them. If you don't have the diamonds, then you're of no use to me or Sophie at this point."

"Don't put this back on me."

He stood up and started toward the entrance, and she hurried to follow.

"Chad, wait. What did you tell them? Where did you tell them the diamonds were?"

Chad kept walking, avoiding her gaze until they were out in the plaza again, but she wasn't finished.

"Chad . . ." She moved in front of him, forcing him to stop. "What did you tell them?"

"I told them I didn't have the diamonds, but I was going to get them. I told them . . . I told them that Rachel had the diamonds. I was just trying to buy myself some time—"

"Your buying yourself time might have gotten her killed!"

"I didn't think they'd find her. And I had no idea you would show up here."

"Wait a minute." The jumbled pieces of the situation had yet to make sense, but something wasn't right. Marcus wasn't the first person who'd told her that she and Rachel could be twins. "They think I'm Rachel."

"I don't know . . . Maybe . . . I think so." She'd never seen him so hesitant. So scared.

She glanced behind her. Maybe Chad wasn't jumping at shadows. They had to be here somewhere. Watching. Waiting. And they thought she was Rachel.

She turned back to Chad. "What happened at Rachel's house that day? Did the person you sent to find the diamonds end up shooting my sister when she walked in on them?"

"No."

"Are you telling me the truth?"

"Yes. I've got to go, Kate." He pulled away from her and headed toward the street in front of the cathedral.

"Not yet, Chad, please . . . There are still too many questions."

She started after him, still not sure about who he'd seen that had spooked him. Still unsure about everything.

Marcus watched Chad slip from the entrance of the church and start toward the busy street. He was walking fast, almost running as he wove between tourists carrying cameras, peddlers asking for money and a group of street performers who were gathering a crowd with their upbeat rap.

Something had spooked Chad.

Kate followed behind him, with Jocelyn, in her gray scarf, just a few steps behind her. Either Kate had managed to scare him or someone was after him. He searched the crowd, trying to figure out what had spooked him.

"He's running," Pierre said.

Marcus picked up his pace. Who was Chad running from?

People exited the church, but no one who fit

any of the descriptions they had. Maybe the man was just being paranoid.

What just happened in there, Kate?

He looked back at where a group of street performers were in front of the cathedral drawing a growing crowd, dancing to the music. Kate had vanished into the crowd behind Chad.

"We're not losing her again . . ."

"She got caught up in the crowd watching the street performance," Jocelyn responded, "but I'm right behind her."

Marcus picked up his pace. "What happened inside there?"

"I don't know. They were sitting on one of the pews, talking, when something spooked him."

"Grab Chad. I'll get Kate."

He spotted her at the edge of the crowd as Chad stumbled off the sidewalk. He called out to her, but there was no way she could hear him above the music.

Marcus saw the truck a second before it hit Chad, but by then it was too late. The driver honked his horn and slammed on his brakes. Chad's body flew like a limp rag doll, before slamming seconds later onto the pavement.

SEVEN

Kate pressed through the crowd that had gathered in front of the church, straining to see where Chad had gone. Music blasted. A horn sounded. Brakes squealed. She turned toward the commotion just in time to see a truck slam into Chad.

"Chad!"

Kate barely heard her own scream above the music entertaining the crowd. She tried to push her way toward the street, straining to see what had happened. He was lying there, still, as the driver exited his car.

Someone grabbed her arm from behind. Instinctively, she tried to pull away as panic whipped through her. Chad had been right. They were here. And they'd found her. Ready to hurt her as they'd hurt her sister and now Chad . . .

"It's okay . . . It's me." Marcus loosened his grip, but didn't let go as he turned her around to face him. Both of his hands rested against her arms as he caught her gaze and pulled her away from the crowd. "Kate?"

"Marcus?" Kate felt a flood of relief surge through her, but even that relief did little to alleviate the fear or the images she couldn't erase from her mind. "Someone just hit Chad. I need to see if he's okay."

"I saw what happened, but I need you to come with me."

"No. I can't. Not yet." She tried to pull away from Marcus's grip. The flow of traffic had yet to stop, as the crowd of spectators turned their attention to the accident. "I can't just leave. I need to see if he's okay."

"Pierre and Jocelyn are there and the police will be here shortly. I don't want you out there, Kate. It's too exposed. Not until I know you're safe. Not until I know exactly what happened."

"What happened?" Her mind struggled to follow his reasoning. "My brother-in-law was hit by a truck . . ."

She paused, realizing what he was thinking. What if it wasn't an accident? What if someone had attempted to kill Chad as they'd tried to kill Rachel?

But why? Nothing made sense.

Marcus pulled her back toward the shadows of the towering church, stopping close to the cold stone structure. "Until I know if that was an accident or not, you need to stay out of sight. We need to get out of here."

Kate hesitated, unable to pull her gaze away from the street. Marcus was right. Someone was after Chad. And that someone—if they thought she was Rachel—was now after her. The music stopped. In its place, sirens screamed in the distance. She could still see Chad's form lying on the ground in front of the taxi. Blood pooled from his head. The driver waved his hands around, shouting something she couldn't understand.

He had told them Rachel had the diamonds.

They thought she was Rachel.

They'd tried to grab her . . .

Kate shivered in the warm afternoon sun, not wanting to continue putting the pieces together. "He hasn't moved, Marcus . . ."

Her heart raced. Her head throbbed. How could she simply walk away? Chad had answers to her questions. Something had spooked him, and she needed to know what.

Marcus tipped her chin slightly, until she was forced to catch his gaze. "You have to trust someone. I need you to trust me. We need to go."

She swallowed hard, knowing she was panicking and not thinking straight. Marcus wasn't the bad guy in this situation. He was only trying to help. And at the moment, she clearly needed all the help she could get.

Marcus pulled her toward him, his hands on her shoulders. "I'm going to keep you safe, Kate. I promise."

She couldn't see Chad anymore because of the growing crowd that had formed around the accident scene. She had to know what happened, and it was more than that. Chad had been in contact with Sophie's kidnappers. Without the diamonds, without Chad, they'd lost their connection to finding her.

"He has information about Sophie," Kate said slowly. "They have her."

"I want you to tell me everything he said to you, but not here. Pierre and Jocelyn will make sure he gets to the hospital, and will speak with him as soon as they can."

Kate felt Marcus pull her the opposite direction. He was touching his ear and talking to someone as they hurried away. Giving orders. Calm. Focused.

I want to know if that was an attack or an accident . . . Go with him to the hospital . . . He might be our only witness.

Her heart was racing too fast. The adrenaline pumping too rapidly. *She'd* been a witness, at least to the accident. She'd watched him step out onto the street. He'd been hit before she could scream. Had hit the ground before she could even react. No matter what Chad had done, or what he'd gotten involved in, Rachel loved Chad. How had things spun so violently out of control?

"Did you see someone following you?"

"No, but it's possible. They think I'm Rachel, and that I know where the diamonds are."

She searched the crowd one last time, the fear in her gut spreading as she recognized him. Chad

had been right. "He's here, Marcus. The bald one who tried to grab me."

Marcus snatched her hand. "Then we need to lose him. Now." Tears stung her eyes, causing the Parisian setting to blur together, as they started across a bridge spanning the Seine near the church. She could still see the faces of the men who'd tried to grab her. Felt them watching her this morning, but she'd prayed it was simply her imagination. Now she knew she hadn't imagined seeing him again. He knew who she was. Knew her sister and Sophie. Knew how to get to her.

If they thought she was involved—thought she had the diamonds—they weren't going to stop looking for her. They'd try to grab her again.

"He's still back there."

Marcus nodded. He was talking to his team again. Advising them to find the man while he got her to safety.

As they waited with a crowd of pedestrians before crossing the busy street, she tried to focus on the row of apartments above a café, with their wrought-iron balconies. The pavement beneath her feet. Anything but that too-vivid image of what she'd just seen. Chad running into the street. Chad being hit by the truck. Chad lying on the ground in a pool of blood . . . And now the added reality that without Chad and the diamonds, she had no idea how she would find Sophie.

She glanced behind her as they wove their way

past souvenir shops selling T-shirts, backpacks and fridge magnets. Surely there was safety on the crowded streets. Busy cafés with people drinking coffee and enjoying a late lunch. But brazen enough to grab her off the street? Brazen enough to kill Chad in broad daylight?

The answer to those questions sent shivers of fear down her spine.

She struggled to keep up with Marcus, feeling as if they were walking in circles through the narrow side streets. Her heart felt numb. The only thing she could feel was the protection of his hand firmly around hers. As if they were a couple on a stroll through the most romantic city in the world. Paris was everything she'd imagined it to be, but this wasn't how she'd expected to spend her time here.

Marcus paused in front of a postcard rack outside a souvenir shop and picked up a photo of Notre Dame.

Kate glanced at the woman sorting through T-shirts beside them. "Why are we stopping?"

"I think we lost him."

He dropped the postcard back into the slot, then grabbed another one, looking as if he had nothing more on his mind than buying a cheap souvenir. But a deeper look into those blue eyes of his proved to her he was clearly on alert.

Fear gripped tighter as the postcard he held blurred in front of her. She blinked, trying to convince herself she was safe with him no matter who was out there. He grabbed her hand and guided her across another street. A minute later, they strolled into a small park that was almost empty, questions still refusing to leave her alone.

Had someone purposefully tried to kill Chad?

No . . . she had to be right. It had to have been an accident. They wanted the diamonds and expected him to get them.

"We'll stop here, but only for a few minutes," Marcus said finally.

"Are you sure?"

He nodded as he led her to an empty bench and sat down beside her. "We'll be safe here for the moment until I hear from Pierre. And in the meantime, I need information."

Kate glanced around her. After the sea of people around the church, the quiet park was a welcome relief. "Okay."

"I need to know exactly what Chad said to you," he said.

Kate gripped the edge of the stone bench with her fingers, not ready to answer his question. All she could think about was Chad. That he'd been hit. That he might be dead. That the marriage Rachel had tried to save might be over. That Sophie might not have a father anymore.

Her head spun. She didn't want to think about any of those things right now.

She glanced across the open square with its

well-trimmed trees, walkways, green lawns and a bronze fountain in the center. Notre Dame loomed in the distance, too close. She could hear the traffic, but the trees and hedges surrounding the square helped muffle the sounds.

"Is Paris where you learned to speak French?" she asked.

"French?" Marcus rested his hands against his thighs and shook his head. "I . . . Yes. I spent two years studying abroad here in Paris thanks to my grandfather. What does that have to do with Chad?"

"Everything . . . Nothing." She wasn't sure what he wanted from her. She didn't have the answers he needed, and after speaking with Chad all she had was more questions. Which was why all she really wanted was for this to be over.

"I don't understand," he prodded.

She looked up at him, trying to curb her frustration. "Of course you don't understand. You're used to asking the right questions and finding the answers. Investigating until you discover the truth, aren't you? You shove aside the feelings and stick to facts and numbers and everything that is concrete. But you don't feel, because if you started feeling then you might realize that there's a person on the other side of the question. That there's a little girl out there who's scared, right now. She misses her mother and everything familiar."

"Whoa." He shifted toward her. "Last time I checked, we were on the same side. I know what has happened today has been traumatic, but I need to know what Chad said because it might help us to find Sophie."

Kate closed her eyes, trying to escape the pictures that kept repeating over and over in her mind. She wasn't being fair to him. He was doing everything he could to not only find Sophie, but to keep her safe, as well. What happened to Chad wasn't his fault.

"I know, and I'm sorry."

But she'd still rather be asking Marcus questions about his grandfather and why he'd decided to come to Paris. Even that distraction, though, wouldn't be enough. Her mind refused to stop replaying what had happened. The sound of the horn and the brakes. The truck tossing Chad like a rag doll.

If he died . . .

"Kate . . . I know this is difficult, but I need you to focus. I need your help."

"It . . . it had to have been an accident." She looked up at Marcus. An ant crawled across his shoulder. She reached up to brush it away, then pulled back her hand. Somehow, the gesture seemed far too . . . intimate.

He leaned forward, not seeming to realize her discomfort. "Why do you think it was an accident?"

"Why would they kill him at this point?" She drew in a ragged breath, still watching the entrances of the park in case the bald man managed to figure out where they were. "He told me they're asking for a ransom. They wouldn't want him dead before they got what they're demanding."

"What are they demanding?"

Kate breathed in, filling her lungs and trying to steady her breathing. "They want the diamonds he stole from them. If they expect him to get the diamonds, they need to keep him alive."

He touched his thumb against her chin and turned her face toward him, bringing her focus back to his face. She stared at him. His eyes were so blue. Like sapphires. "Did he tell you where Sophie is?"

She shook her head. "He said they want to exchange her for the diamonds he stole, but he doesn't have them."

"Where are they?"

"He sent them to Rachel. Inside music boxes for Sophie. Five millions dollars' worth."

Marcus let out a low whistle. "He *was* smuggling them."

Kate nodded. "The music boxes were expensive. Rachel thought he was trying to buy Sophie's affection. Rachel tried to make Chad understand that she didn't want things from him . . . She simply wanted him. She mailed them—I'd assumed to Chad—but when I spoke to him, he insisted he didn't have them."

"We need to speak with your sister. We need to know where she sent them."

"I spoke with my mother a few hours ago, and she was still unconscious. She promised to let me know if there were any changes."

"Did he tell you anything else?"

"That he was supposed to meet them at the Eiffel Tower to exchange the diamonds for Sophie."

"And they think you're Rachel?"

Kate pressed her lips together and nodded.

"Which explains why they tried to grab you," Marcus continued. "Do you believe him? Is there any chance he's lying and he's the one who has his daughter?"

"He's made some foolish choices, but I don't think he'd risk Sophie's life. Even for a fortune."

Marcus shook his head as he caught her gaze. "If you ask me, that's exactly what he's done."

EIGHT

Marcus looked at Kate. Her face had paled. Her eyes were rimmed with tears. Between jet lag, fear of losing her sister and niece, and now Chad's accident, he was amazed she hadn't already completely fallen apart.

He shoved his hands into his front pockets, and stood, then stared out across the quiet, manicured space. He was pushing her too hard. Forgot that she wasn't used to the grueling pace needed in an investigation. And managed to forget she might have lost her sister and was fighting to find her niece.

Guilt surfaced. When had he become so desensitized to the emotional side of his cases and their victims? To the lives of the people involved and not just his relentless determination to ensure the bad guys paid?

Because Kate Elliot wasn't just another case he needed to solve and check off. She was a woman who loved her family. Who was willing to risk whatever it took to find her niece, even if it meant risking his wrath and, even more important, her own life. And in turn, his protective instincts had kicked in. That deep, inbred need to protect her. And a matching determination to ensure he did just that.

He turned back toward her and took a moment to study her face again. She was beautiful in a classic, timeless way. But that wasn't what was throwing him off. Maybe he'd spent too much time around jaded coworkers, or interrogating criminals, but there was something different about her. Despite her tendency not to listen to his advice, she had a sincere, straightforward honesty, along with a willingness to put herself at risk for the sake of someone else.

She was—in a word—refreshing. And as much as he didn't want to admit it, he liked that. Too much.

He rubbed the back of his neck, trying to ease the tension that was spreading down his back. Because she was right. Interrogating her like a suspect wasn't going to help either of them find Sophie. Or help him close his case. What she didn't realize, though, was that time was crucial and the longer it took for them to find out the truth, the greater the risk to Sophie's life.

He'd seen people risk the lives of family members for far less than a cache of diamonds. It always amazed him how quickly the lure of money could change a person.

Besides that, they were getting nowhere. She was in shock, which was normal, but she was going to have to pull herself together. They needed answers, and he needed her help to find them. But even so, maybe he was taking the wrong approach.

Marcus sat back down beside Kate on the park bench. “You asked earlier where we are. The name of this square is René-Viviani.”

Kate’s eyes widened in question, as if she were unsure where he was going with the comment.

“I used to come here quite a bit when I lived in Paris,” he continued, “along with a few other parks, mainly for the solitude. The view of Notre Dame looming in the background was one of the draws to this park. The cathedral is such an incredible piece of architecture.”

“It is beautiful.”

“That,” he said, pointing to a leaning, gnarled tree, “is said to be the oldest living tree in Paris. It’s a variety of the locust tree, and is well over 400 years old. The park was opened in the late 1920s and named after René Viviani, who was the prime minister of France during the first year of World War I.”

Her slight smile brought out the dimples in her cheeks, but she still didn’t look convinced that he was on her side. “Is this one of your interrogation tactics? A bit of good cop thrown into the interrogation mix?”

“It’s not a tactic.” He focused his attention on her while still keeping his senses on high alert, certain that whoever was looking for Kate hadn’t given up their quest. “I know the past couple days have been difficult, and I realize I'm pushing you hard. This case has been difficult. And for you, extremely personal."

"Very." She nodded then jutted her chin toward the middle of the square. "What do you know about the sculpture?"

"Part of it represents pieces of the legend of St. Julien, the church adjacent to the park."

"And the infants?" she asked. "Some seem to have wings, while others appear . . . almost lifeless."

"During the time that France was working with Nazi Germany, more than 11,000 infants were deported to Auschwitz. The infants represent a hundred or so of those children who lived in this vicinity."

"Wow." The sadness in her eyes was back. "That's horrible."

"Yes, it is."

She fiddled with a broken nail for a moment, before looking back up at him. "So if this isn't an interrogation tactic—good cop, bad cop—why the sudden switch to tour-guide mode?"

He hesitated before answering her question, afraid his actions were being guided too much by emotions instead of his head. "You've managed to remind me that while it's still important, this case isn't only about finding justice."

"What's it about, then?"

He resisted the urge to push back a strand of hair

that the wind had blown across her check. "It's about a woman who loves her family, and who will do anything it takes to ensure their safety."

She folded her hands in her lap and shook her head. "What I've done is nothing more than anyone else would do in a situation like this."

"I'm not so sure. You've shown an incredible amount of courage and guts."

Her laugh rang hollow. "I can honestly tell you that I'm not feeling particularly courageous at the moment. My instincts at the church were to run when Chad told me he thought someone was after me."

"What made you stay?"

"Believing he had answers I needed. Family *is* important to me. And I promised my sister I'd find Sophie."

He studied her expression. There was fatigue in her eyes and that hint of sadness, but he didn't miss the spark of determination in them, as well. No matter how hard he wanted to fight the feeling, he wanted to know more about her. More than just the answer to what made her fly five thousand miles to take on a possible murderer.

He wanted to know if she was a morning person or a night owl. What her parents did for a living. What was on her bucket list? Did she like to cook? Did she prefer dogs or cats? When was her birthday . . . ?

"Tell me about your family." Marcus spoke the

comment out loud before he'd had a chance to consider the consequences.

"I'm sorry?" she asked.

He was fumbling again, which wasn't like the orderly, methodical way he normally functioned. Maybe he was somewhat desensitized, but there were reasons for that. He shouldn't be trying to get to know her on a personal level. But why, then, had his heart stepped in, aching to get involved?

"Start with yourself." He cleared his throat, wanting to start over and salvage things. "We might have to wait a bit until they call back with news about Chad. I'd like to know more about you as a person, not just as someone in my protection. You mentioned you'd been to Africa?"

She looked up at him with those wide, hazel eyes. "I . . . I went to work on a wildlife documentary. The project was connected with a conservation program in South Africa, the Chizoba Predator Project."

"What animals were you researching?"

"We spent eight months tracking a lion family and documenting the dynamics within the pride."

"Wow. It must have been fascinating."

"It was."

It didn't take much for him to imagine her out in an open jeep, camera in hand, lions playing close by. But today, she was sitting beside him, the breeze catching her hair, and the hint of coconut and flowers of her perfume filling his senses.

Maybe getting to know her better hadn't been one of his better ideas, but neither was he willing to stop. Not just yet. The real reason they were here, together, hadn't changed at all. But for the moment, maybe the reality of everything they were facing could wait.

"So you enjoyed your work there?" he continued.

"Africa . . ." Her shoulders dropped slightly, and her hands unclenched in her lap as if she were finally starting to relax. "It changed my life. I loved the documentary work and always planned to continue in that line of work."

"What changed?"

"We ended up spending some of our free time working in a couple of the local schools. We were able to join a group made up from the community who helped ensure students had the supplies and uniforms they needed. We also threw a couple parties for them, and in getting to know some of them, I realized how much I enjoyed relating to kids. And that maybe, with some training, I could find a way to make a difference."

"Do you plan to go back and work there?"

"One day, maybe, but I've gone back to school for now. I'm getting a degree in counseling."

"From what I know about you, I think you'd be a great counselor. You clearly have a heart for people."

A smile played on her lips at the compliment as she looked up at him. "I have a good friend who runs a nonprofit for at-risk teens. I'm planning to join her as soon as I finish school. I might not be able to save the world, but I'd like to at least try to make a difference for some local kids."

Marcus caught the passion in her voice. She was verbalizing what he'd felt when he'd first started working for the agency. But it was more than that. Most of the women he'd gone out with lately—not that there had been very many after Nicole—seemed far more concerned with their careers and status. He'd listened to them go on and on about their lives. They'd had very little to say about making a difference in the lives of others.

Apparently, he'd been looking in the wrong places. Not that he was looking. But if he were . . .

"When I started working for the FBI, I jumped in, believing I could save the world. Maybe I've seen too much of the dark side of our society." He paused, surprised at his confession. "Lately, I just hoped to make a dent for good. But most of the time, it seems as if I arrest one person, only to find out that someone else has taken their place."

Kate shook her head, unaware of how the sun caught the blondish-red highlights in her hair. Or how her genuineness was managing to cut through every defense he'd managed to erect the past few years.

"I'm trying not to look at life that way," she said. "I saw enough suffering during my time in Africa to make me realize that as much as I want to, I will never be able to *fix* everything. I'm just hoping to make a difference in the lives of individuals. It might not save the world, but it will make a difference for that one person."

Kate sat beside Marcus, picking at a broken nail, worried she sounded pious or arrogant. She'd meant what she said, but that didn't mean that she didn't struggle over the fact that she couldn't fix everything. Like what was happening to her family right now. She was coming to realize that as much as she wanted to, she really couldn't fix everything.

And on top of that, the fear she'd felt over the past few days had yet to dissipate. Fear over losing her sister. Fear over losing Sophie. Fear over the knowledge that someone believed she had information about the diamonds.

But beyond that fear, she was also feeling something else. Marcus made her believe she was safe when he was with her. That he was worth trusting. That he'd do whatever it took to protect her.

Trust had never come without complications for her. And after Kevin, even considering trusting the man sitting beside her was saying a lot. Maybe she didn't have a choice. But part of her wanted to believe that he could keep her safe. That he could find Sophie.

One thing was clearly true in her mind. Marcus

wasn't anything like the man who had left her at the altar. Kevin had been a coward, unable to come to her with the truth of how he felt, but Marcus was anything but a coward. Already, she'd seen him risk his life for her and for justice.

"You okay?" he asked, pulling her out of her thoughts.

"I will be as soon as this is over." Kate pressed her lips together. "Thank you."

"For what?"

"For understanding that I'm struggling to deal with all of this. That I need time to process what has happened."

She wanted to add that she enjoyed talking with him about something besides the case, even though she knew that not dealing with what had just happened to Chad was doing nothing more than postponing it.

Because the threat was never far away. They were out there. Somewhere. And had made it clear that they were determined to get what they were after.

"Tell me about your family, then," he continued. "Not with me as an agent, just . . . a friend."

Kate turned her gaze away from those intense blue eyes of his that made her want to explore the idea of a relationship with Marcus O'Brian beyond agent and *just* a friend. Just as she was about to open up, Marcus's phone rang. He took the call and signaled for her to wait a second.

Reality hit her all at once as he stood and turned away from her. The flower beds she'd admired earlier, with their yellow, orange and pink blooms, began to blur along with the couple lying on the grass, and the student eating his lunch.

They were out there. Somewhere. Determined. Focused. Looking for her. Thinking she had the diamonds. Believing she was Rachel.

"That was Pierre," Marcus said, sitting back down beside her.

"Have they been able to speak to Chad yet?" Kate's breath caught. Something was wrong. She could see it in his eyes.

"He and Jocelyn are at the hospital, where they were hoping to speak to him in person—"

"What's wrong, Marcus?"

"I'm sorry, Kate. I don't know how else to tell you, but straight-out. He died just after arriving at the hospital. The emergency doctors tried to revive him, but the damage from the impact was too extensive."

She fought to catch her breath. Fought to take in the news. Chad might have hurt her sister, but she didn't want him dead. And he was the link to Sophie. Without him . . .

She wiped away a tear. "How do I tell Rachel that he's dead? How do I tell Sophie that she's lost her father?"

"I know this is hard, Kate, but you're strong. I saw that the first time I met you at your sister's house. And you'll get through this one day at a time."

"And in the meantime? He was our connection to Sophie." She shook her head. "What do we do now?"

"Since we can't question Chad, there's only one thing I know that will put an end to this." He reached out and squeezed her hand. "We need to meet Pierre and Jocelyn back at the safe house and regroup. Because we have to track down those diamonds."

NINE

Kate followed Marcus out of the safe haven of the René-Viviani. Part of her wanted to stay, because for a few brief minutes, she'd been able to forget the reality of the situation they were facing. Getting to know Marcus on a personal level had been unexpected yet welcome. Because despite the seriousness of what was going on around them, he managed to calm the storm raging through her—even if only temporarily.

But that *reality* now loomed again in front of her as real and tangible as the Notre Dame Cathedral to her left. Five million dollars had motivated someone to shoot Rachel and grab Sophie. Five million dollars had provoked someone to try to grab her off the streets. And while she still didn't understand everything that had happened, the threat was very real. Someone was out there looking for her. Someone who would stop at nothing to find her and the diamonds.

As far as she knew, though, the trail of the diamonds ended when Rachel mailed the music boxes. And there was a good chance that whoever she mailed them to didn't even know what was contained in the packages. She was certain Rachel hadn't known Chad's ulterior motive in sending Sophie the music boxes. Or how those seemingly innocent gifts would in turn cost her her family.

Marcus grabbed her hand to help maneuver her through the crowded intersection, his touch bringing with it the needed reminder that she wasn't alone. As they headed away from Notre Dame, past shops and cafés, the pedestrian traffic began to lighten. Apartment buildings lined each side of the narrow street that was lined with cars and rows of bicycles. Motorcycles zipped past them down the one-way street, along with the constant flow of cars and delivery trucks.

"There's a metro station not too far from here," he said finally. "It's the quickest way to get back to the apartment."

Kate shivered despite the warm afternoon sun.

"You okay?" he asked, still holding her hand.

Kate tried to suppress the feelings of panic. "You'll think I'm silly if I tell you."

"I can think of a lot of descriptions of you, but silly isn't one of them."

"When I was ten," she began, "I went to New York on a family vacation with my parents."

"And you took the subway?"

She nodded. "Up to that moment, I'd loved everything about New York City. My dad decided it might be our only trip to the Big Apple, so he let us do everything, starting with Times Square, the Statue of Liberty and the

Metropolitan Museum of Art. He took us to the top of the Empire State Building, Central Park, a Broadway play and even a Yankees game. My sister and I thought we'd died and gone to heaven. After living in a small town in Texas our entire lives, New York was indescribable."

"So what happened on the subway?" he asked.

Memories surfaced as they walked past an outdoor café where an older couple chatted over cups of coffee at a table for two, seemingly unaware of anyone around them. She shot Marcus a sideways glance, feeling the warmth and protection of his fingers entwined with hers and wondering if she'd find someone to spend the next fifty years of her life with. She shook her head and pushed away the thought. When this was over, Marcus would take on another dangerous case with the FBI, and she'd go back to her quiet, suburban life where things like kidnappings and ransoms and five million dollars' worth of diamonds didn't exist.

"There were so many people around me," Kate said, going back to his question. "I remember I could hardly breathe, and I can still smell the sewer and garbage from that moment. I stood there, my eyes closed, trying to hold my breath, and when I opened them the doors of the subway were shutting and my parents were gone."

"You lost them?"

"I don't think I've ever been so frightened—until the past few days, at least. It was dark in the car and lights kept flashing while people kept pushing into me."

"What did you do?"

"I found a seat and sat down in that car until the end of the line, terrified. Somehow I finally got off and was found by a police officer, who made some calls and was eventually able to find my very frantic parents. But since then . . ."

"You've managed to avoid underground transportation."

She nodded, hearing the foolishness of her actions in his words.

"It will take longer, but we could walk," he offered.

"No, you're right. The subway is quicker." She wanted to be back in that safe house as soon as possible. But she also didn't want to be defeated by fear. "It will be fine."

Kate tried to shake off the feeling. She wasn't ten. And this time she had Marcus.

She shook her head as she took in a deep breath. "I told you it was silly."

"And like I said, considering the way you're handling what's going on right now, I still say you're brave."

Marcus pressed his hand against the small of her back as they took the narrow flight of stairs into the belly of the city. He had somehow become her constant in a world that seemed to have spun out of control. The one person who seemed to stand between her and the terror awaiting her on the other side. Someone jostled against her and she grabbed Marcus's arm as he bought her ticket, then guided her toward the turnstile.

The subway on the other side of the platform zoomed down the tunnel while they waited for theirs to arrive among the dozens of passengers. She didn't feel brave. Part of her still felt like the ten-year-old who'd somehow managed to lose her parents in the middle of New York City.

Even now, everyone seemed to know exactly where they were going. Except for her. She still remembered studying the map of the underground city on her tiptoes until a police officer had approached her. For months after that, getting lost had been a constant fear.

Today fear wrapped around her from a different source. Marcus seemed to know the system as well as any Parisian, but this time it was more than her panic over the city's subway. Someone was still after her. She was certain of it. She studied the crowd, aware of every person in the growing crowd. Of every person exiting their subway car, certain she would find him lurking in the shadows.

She watched for him as they crowded onto the subway, and as the doors swished closed behind them with Marcus's arm now wrapped tightly around her waist. But no matter how hard she tried, she couldn't shake the reality that someone was determined to find her. And that there was nothing they could do to stop it.

With no place to sit, they stood beside one of the metal poles in the middle of the train. Marcus drew his arm tighter around her waist as the car pulled out of the station and plunged them into the darkness of the tunnel. Lights flickered above them. Panic threatened to take over.

She studied a young woman with two children. A baby cried in the back. An older man dozed in one of the seats. The train was packed with commuters on their way home from work. Most ignored those around them, reading a newspaper or dozing. None of them seemed to notice she was standing in the middle of the train screaming on the inside. They'd found her before, but she was safe now. All they needed to do was find the diamonds—and Sophie—and this nightmare would be over.

"You okay?" Marcus asked above the noise.

Kate nodded.

"We're the third stop."

She shifted her focus to the map on the train's wall as they sped down the tunnel. Three more stops, and they could get off. Three more stops, and she'd be safe again.

Do not fear, for I am with you.

Do not be dismayed, for I am your God.

The words from Isaiah she'd memorized years ago started running through her mind.

I will strengthen and help you.

Do not fear.

Do not fear.

She repeated the words until she felt a small wave of peace sweep over her. She could do this—she would do this—whatever it took, for Rachel and Sophie.

Leaning into Marcus as new passengers pressed into the train, she grasped on to that sliver of peace and kept praying. Prayed for continued peace. For wisdom. For protection. For healing for Rachel . . .

Kate's fingers tightened around the pole as the train left the platform and she looked out across the crowded car. Her breath caught. He was standing at the far end, near the door. She recognized him immediately. Bald head, tattooed arm sleeves and those gray eyes that seemed to pierce straight through her. Panic engulfed her as their eyes met.

Do not be afraid.

She couldn't breathe. Couldn't move. She was ten again. Alone, lost and afraid. She counted to ten and tried to stomp out the fear. He still hadn't moved. Maybe he hadn't seen her. Maybe it really wasn't him. She closed her eyes for a moment. Or maybe she'd imagined him. But a moment later, when she glanced again across the crowded train, he was still there.

Do not be afraid.

She nudged Marcus and leaned toward him. “He’s here. At the far end of the car on the left.”

He grabbed her hand and squeezed her fingers. “Okay. At the next stop we’re getting off. Stay close to me.”

She tightened her grip around the strap of her purse, forcing herself not to look back at the tattooed man. Trying to convince herself she would be safe with Marcus. But even with the strapping agent beside her, her confidence was fading.

God, I don’t know when this is going to be over. How much more of this I can take . . .

Because whoever was behind this had proved they weren’t simply playing a game of threats. And that fact alone had her wanting to run for her life.

She glanced up. This time the tattooed man caught her gaze. Panic struck again. Her fingers gripped Marcus’s arm. This was no coincidence. He knew she was here and as foolish as it seemed, he clearly had no plans of letting a crowd stop him.

She tried to walk through their options. He could be armed, but security appeared to be tight, even at the metro stations. They could get off, find a police officer. Surely that would deter the man.

Marcus pressed through the crowd toward the doors as the train prepared to stop. Seconds later, a rush of commuters stepped out onto the platform with them. Kate glanced back, trying to find him. He'd vanished into the crowd.

"Is he following us?"

"I don't know. I lost him."

But she knew he was still there. She had no idea how, but in a sea of people, he'd managed to find her again. She searched behind her while struggling to keep up with Marcus across the congested platform. He *was* still there. She knew it.

"Do you know where we are?" she asked, out of breath.

"More or less."

His answer didn't help alleviate the panic. She glanced behind her again at a group of women wearing colorful saris, and found him.

"He's there. Twenty yards or so behind us."

Marcus gripped her hand tighter and pulled her toward the exit, pushing through the crowd, past an elderly man playing an accordion. Past ads for shampoo and movies. Past the stairs that led to the street.

"Where are we going?"

"Back onto the platform on the other side. If we time it right we'll be able to lose him on the next train that comes through."

She nodded. Marcus should go after the man,

but he clearly wasn't taking any chances because of her. She glanced again. He was still behind them, but they'd managed to lengthen the distance between them.

A whoosh of wind came down the tunnel just before the train arrived on the other platform. Her heart pounded in her chest as the doors flew open and Marcus pulled her onto the train. Seconds later, the doors swooshed shut behind them, leaving their opponent on the platform.

Marcus led her to a pair of open seats and slid in beside her. "We lost him, Kate."

She searched the car, which was less crowded this time. His plan had worked. She was safe again. For the moment.

He still had her hand. "It's going to be okay."

She shook her head, legs shaking, her lip quivering. She tried to remind herself that this wasn't like the last time. Marcus was here. He was going to make sure the people behind this paid for what they had done.

Kate's phone rang as they sped through the tunnel. She pulled it out of her pocket, hoping it was an update from her mom on Rachel. She needed answers from her sister. She glanced at the caller ID. *Caller unknown.*

She glanced up at Marcus before answering the call. Who else would be calling her?

"Hello?"

"Don't talk. Just listen or your niece is dead."

Kate fumbled with the phone and almost dropped it. No. It was nothing more than a bluff. They wanted the diamonds and were desperate.

"Kate?" Marcus prompted.

She held her hand over the phone. "It's him."

"Ask him where Sophie is."

"Where's my niece?" Kate heard the desperation in her voice as she asked the question.

"We know Chad is dead. If you want to see Sophie alive, be on the second level of the Eiffel Tower with the diamonds tomorrow at noon. Come alone. No games. It's the same deal we had with Chad. Otherwise, I can guarantee you'll never see her alive again."

"You need to buy time, Kate," Marcus said.

"Wait . . . I'll get them for you, but . . . it's going to take me time."

There was a long pause on the line. "You've got until noon on Friday."

Marcus's hand brushed across her shoulder. That still gave them less than forty-eight hours. They would simply have to find a way to make it work. "Tell them we need a photo. Proof that she's okay."

Kate swallowed hard. "We need proof of life."

"We'll send you a photo."

The line went dead.

Kate cradled the phone between her hands. A week ago, she'd gone with Rachel and Sophie to the party store to plan Sophie's fifth birthday.

They'd picked plates and napkins to go with the princess theme. Kate had gone back later and bought the tiara Sophie had fallen in love with. It was still sitting in Kate's front room, in a pink-and-white gift bag with sparkly tissue paper.

Keep her safe, God. Please. I don't know what else to do. Don't know what will happen if Mom and I lose both of them.

Her phone beeped. Kate clicked on the message. The photo opened. Sophie sat cross-legged on a small wooden chair, her expression serious. She held Lily, her one-eyed bunny, in one hand. In the other, she held a newspaper. Kate zoomed in on the paper. June 14. Today's date. She felt her lungs exhale. Sophie was alive . . . for now. And they had less than forty-eight hours to find the diamonds and ensure she stayed alive.

TEN

Marcus breathed a sigh of relief as he stepped into the safe house behind Kate. They needed to track down the man they'd encountered on the subway, but not at the risk of Kate's life. In the meantime, a BOLO was out on the man, ensuring Interpol, Homeland Security and the FBI were all on the lookout for him. All Marcus could do now was pray that would be enough to find him quickly.

Which left him coming back to the same question again. How was he supposed to keep Kate safe and do his job at the same time? The only answer he'd come up with so far was to keep her in the safe house until all of this was over. And while he had a feeling she wasn't going to like it, as far as he was concerned, it was their only option. Because if it weren't for the fact he needed her help, he'd already have sent her home.

With Rachel still in ICU and Chad dead, Kate was the closest thing he had to a source. And at least here, he could keep an eye on her instead of relying on someone else for her safety. His jaw tensed. Which shouldn't matter on a personal level. But it did. He didn't need to be the one protecting her, but neither could he shake the worry over something else happening to her. And him not being there to save her.

He watched her set her bag onto the small dining room table, before she moved to stand in front of the floor-to-ceiling window overlooking the busy street below. She folded her arms across her chest, the tension in her posture clear as she continued the silence that had settled between them on their way back to the safe house.

"Pierre and Jocelyn will be here about seven with dinner," he said. "That will give us time to go over what we have and make a plan of action for finding the diamonds and making the exchange."

A plan that ensured she stayed out of danger.

Kate nodded.

"I'd still like your help in going through your sister's photos and journal, so hopefully we can find a clue as to where she might have sent them."

He waited for her earlier anger to return over the reminder that he'd read through Rachel's journal, but instead, she simply nodded.

"Do you know Jocelyn's story?" she asked after another long pause had settled between them. "She told me she volunteered for this case. Told me it was personal, but she didn't tell me why."

Marcus raised his brow slightly at the question. "I've seen photos of her family she left behind in the Central African Republic. For years, rebels controlled much of the diamond-producing areas. Most of her family was murdered in the conflict that was funded primarily by those diamonds. She escaped with her mother to France when she was thirteen."

"And her father?"

"I believe he died in the mines a few years later." Marcus stepped next to her in front of the window, where the early-evening sun cast long shadows across the hardwood floors of the apartment. "Why all the questions about Jocelyn? I trust her and Pierre completely if that's what you're worried about."

"No. I trust her, too." Kate continued staring out the window. "I'm just trying to put together all the pieces of the puzzle. Tell me what you know about the diamond smuggling Chad was involved in."

"We call it Operation Solitaire. Diamonds are being smuggled into the US in exchange for military-grade weapons in a number of third-world African and Middle Eastern countries."

"So the diamonds play a role in the succession of rebels as they use the gems to fund the conflict."

Marcus nodded. "That's a pretty good summary. We found compelling evidence during our investigation that Chad was working as one of the buyers. He bought the diamonds off the books from countries like the CAR, where Jocelyn is from, then sold them after they were cut and polished."

"What about the embargoes on blood diamonds? Isn't that supposed to stop things like this from happening?"

"There are embargoes in place, but people still manage to smuggle them from one country to another."

"How?"

He studied her expression. She was processing everything he was telling her. Trying to make sense of a situation that wasn't adding up. He'd seen the same reaction from people whose lives had suddenly been turned upside-down because of a tragedy. Being innocent didn't mean you stayed immune to the consequences of other people's actions.

"Diamonds are easier to smuggle than drugs and weapons," he explained. "Metal detectors don't pick them up. There is nothing for the drug-sniffing dogs to smell. I've heard of people swallowing them, or simply putting them in their wallet."

"Can't they be traced?" she asked.

"Once they're cut and polished, it's almost impossible to determine the origin of a stone. Even with the Kimberley Process and its regulations, some estimate that as high as 15 percent of diamonds sold are actually conflict diamonds."

"And the Kimberley Process? What's its role?"

"They are the world's diamond watchdog whose goal it is to stem the flow of rough diamonds to rebel movements. But even with their regulations in place, there are still countries like the Central African Republic and the Democratic Republic of Congo where much of the fighting can be linked to the control of minerals."

Marcus answered her questions, knowing those answers were an important step for her in trying to make sense of her niece's disappearance. If situations like this could ever be made sense of.

"So Chad skimmed diamonds that should have gone to his buyer, and in turn made some people up the ladder very angry when they realized he was skimming his own share off the top," she said.

"Yes."

Angry enough to shoot Rachel and kidnap Sophie.

She turned to face him. Her eyes were rimmed with tears, but despite everything that had happened, they hadn't lost their look of determination. Which was good. She was going to need that determination to get through the days to come.

"I've been thinking about Sophie and the exchange," she began.

He cocked his head and frowned. "What exactly have you been thinking about?"

"I need to be the one who makes the exchange for Sophie."

"Kate—"

“Hear me out, Marcus, because I know what you’re going to say. They told *me* to show up at the Eiffel Tower. That I was to be the one who makes the exchange. I need to do this, Marcus. I *have* to do this.”

“Forget it.” As far as he was concerned, her staying out of the exchange was nonnegotiable. “It’s too dangerous, Kate. You have no experience in a situation like this, where even a well-executed plan can go wrong. I’m not prepared to risk your life unnecessarily. We can still get Sophie back—”

“I’m willing to take a risk, because they told me to be there.”

“Trust me, they’re more interested in the diamonds than the deliverer. And the bottom line is that it’s a dangerous game, Kate. We’ll make a plan, expect the unexpected and pray for the best outcome. That’s all we can do.”

She grabbed her phone out of her pocket and held up the photo of Sophie she’d put as her wallpaper in front of him. The photo of the adorable four-year-old with her pigtails and bright smile tugged at his heart, just as she’d intended.

“Praying for the best outcome is essential,” she said, “but going against Sophie’s captors’ instructions is foolish. I’m not willing to take that chance. We’ve both seen what these people can do.”

“Kate . . .” He paused as she turned back to the

window, because he didn't know what to say. Didn't know what to do to make things right. He wasn't even sure he could make things right. Whoever had taken Sophie was playing a game, but it was a game where there were no set rules.

And what if Kate was right? Was it worth risking her life to save her niece? He knew how she would answer, but he wanted to find a way to ensure both of them stayed safe.

"What do you see?" she asked, interrupting his thoughts.

"What do you mean?"

"Outside this apartment."

His brow furrowed as he moved closer to her. "I don't know . . . Traffic, buildings, people. Why? What do you see?"

"The sun glistening against the rooftop. The red awning over the corner café. The pink flowers in the apartment window across the way. And walking down the street, there's a couple of tourists."

Marcus couldn't help but smile at her observation regarding the tourists. "White tennis shoes, his fanny pack and her *I Love Paris* bag. With your eye for detail, maybe you could be an FBI agent after all."

"I don't think so." She pressed her fingers against the window frame. "As a photographer I've learned to look at the details. Often, in even the most simple setting, you can find amazing beauty. An everyday object shown in a different way with a simple lens change or camera angle can bring beauty to the ordinary."

"You're an optimist," he said, thinking he understood what she was trying to say. She was the one who expected to find the extraordinary in the ordinary. Who found beauty in the world around her despite the difficulties of life.

She turned to him and caught his gaze. "I can normally find the good in situations, but this time . . . this time it's different. I don't know how this game is supposed to be played. And even if I did, I can't change the circumstances of this situation, and that not being in control . . . it scares me."

Marcus struggled for the right words when nothing he could say could change the situation. "Everything you're feeling right now—the anger, the hurt and confusion—they're all normal, Kate."

"Is it normal for a grad student to find herself involved with a bunch of international diamond and gun smugglers?" She shook her head and turned back toward him. "You're right. I am an optimist. I always have faith that things will work out, but this time . . . I don't know. I'm worried about my family. Worried that we made the wrong decision in asking the kidnappers for more time. All we did was prolong her time with whoever has her."

"Come here." He took her hand and led her to the couch, where he sat down next to her. "We didn't have a choice, Kate, because we don't have the diamonds. I'm not even sure the time they gave us is going to be enough to find them."

"We could make a plan." She pulled her hand away from his then clasped them together in her lap. "We could show up at the arranged exchange and snatch her. Arrest her kidnappers."

"It's never that easy, and if the plan went wrong? Exchanges are risky. They're not going to make the switch until they know they're getting the diamonds. It's a delicate balancing act. I know that the waiting is horrid, but we have to do this the right way. And in turn give Sophie her best chance for us getting her back."

"And if we don't find the diamonds in time?"

"We'll find them." He paused, praying he was right. "We'll find them, because we have to."

"Now who's the optimist?" She shot him a half smile despite the tears in her eyes. "But you're right. We *will* find those diamonds, because Sophie's life depends on it."

And Kate was depending on him.

Kate, who was supposed to be nothing more to him than another source in a case.

Except she wasn't *just* a source. Somehow she'd become so much more, and he couldn't help but like her. A lot. And not just as a person who could help him solve his case.

She sniffled, and he handed her a tissue from the side table, then waited for her to blow her nose. He still wasn't sure how it had happened, but from out of the blue she'd managed to walk into his life and tilt his world upside-down. Not to mention what she'd managed to do with his heart. She'd reminded him to look for hope. Made him look beyond the cold details of the case to the individuals involved. To the details that really mattered. And she had him wondering about the possibility of seeing her again after this was all over.

"I'm not finished discussing the exchange, but what I can't do," she continued, "is sit here doing nothing. I need you to let me help."

He cleared his throat and leaned back against the couch. Staying focused had never been an issue for him before Kate. "I need your help, but I intend to keep you safe, too."

"I know." Kate nodded and the tears were back. "I'm just so scared, Marcus. Scared I'm going to lose them both, and I don't know how my mother would handle that. I can't let that happen."

Kate tried to stop the tears pooling in her eyes before they ran down her cheeks. She fanned her face with her hand, embarrassed she'd given in completely to her emotions and broken down. If they were going to find Sophie, she needed to stay strong, because falling apart wasn't going to help anyone. Sophie needed her. Rachel needed her. Even her mother needed her. But right now her head was swimming with all the possible scenarios of things that could go wrong . . . and the urge to simply run.

Because at the moment, being the strong one seemed too hard.

Marcus leaned forward and brushed away the tears from her cheeks. "Hey . . . it's going to be okay."

She looked at him, her vision blurred, wishing she could lean against his chest and sob away the pain. Wishing he would gather her into his arms and help her forget.

"What if it isn't okay?" she asked finally. "What if Rachel dies, or we don't find Sophie. How will I tell my mom? I still need to tell her that Chad is dead, but every time I think about him, all I can see is him lying on the street with blood pooling around his head—"

"Kate—"

"I'm sorry." She tried to erase his concern with the wave of her hand, then reached around him and grabbed another tissue. "This is crazy. Rachel's the crier in the family. I'm the practical one. If it's broke, fix it. If you can't fix it, replace it. It will all be okay eventually."

But this time things might not end up okay, even though she wanted desperately to fix things. She'd hopped on the next flight to Paris to find

Sophie. Ignored Marcus's warnings and probably all her normal common sense. Met with Chad without telling Marcus . . .

"I don't normally blubber, and cry and cause a scene," she continued, before blowing her nose again.

"You need to give yourself some credit, because face it," he said, "you've been through a lot these past few days."

He shifted in his seat beside her, looking uncomfortable. She was certain he'd be more in his element interrogating criminals and suspects than trying to comfort a blubbering female like herself, and wouldn't blame him one bit if *he* decided to run. But instead of running, he took her hands and pulled them toward him, making her heart flutter at his nearness.

"You're right. I can't promise everything will be okay," he said. "But I can promise we will do everything we can to find Sophie. People are praying for your sister, Kate, and while I know God doesn't always fix things the way we think He should, He's still right here. Walking with you each step of the way."

She nodded, wanting to believe him. Wanting to believe everything would be okay.

I know You're there, God, but even that knowledge doesn't always stop me from feeling gripped with the fear. Help me to feel Your presence. To trust You're there.

She looked up at Marcus and studied his face. There was that hint of a five-o'clock shadow, and a concern in his blue eyes that suggested both compassion and unease. She was grateful for the sense of protection and safety he brought, but knew he was right. Even with all of the resources he brought to the table, he couldn't promise everything would be okay.

I can't control this situation, or fix it, for that matter, God. I need You now. Please. Show us what to do.

"Can I share something with you?" he asked.

She nodded, his question pulling her out of her thoughts.

"As you might have noticed, I'm not exactly the emotional type, but we're doing a Bible study in my small men's group at church on David that has had me look at emotion in a different light." He laced their fingers together. "When you read through the Psalms you can't help but see David's deep emotion, and sometimes, even, his fear. There were times when he wept out loud to the point of exhaustion."

Kate considered his words. "I guess I've never thought of David as being afraid. I mean, he faced a giant and killed him when no one else would."

"I don't know, but maybe sometimes, the healthiest thing to do is to simply stop and weep. And that's okay." A shadow crossed Marcus's face. “Loss changes a person. You know that. I know that.”

Marcus’s gaze shifted away from her for a moment. Graphic photographs of crime scenes that would never be erased from his memory flipped through his mind. No matter how much he tried to distance himself, each victim had left a lasting scar he tried daily to erase.

“I suppose you and I are somewhat alike in the emotional department,” he continued. “I was always the older sibling who took care of everyone else. Sometimes it’s hard to be the one who has to carry that burden. Especially when you’re hurting, as well.”

“Yes, it is.” She nudged him with her elbow. “But I suppose having that soft side isn’t so bad.”

“Maybe not, but I’ve always made it a priority to not allow my work to become personal. If I did, I’m not sure how I’d handle most of my cases.” He hesitated. “But there’s something different about this case. Something that makes me want to forget I’m working a case.”

A smile played on the edges of her lips. “Meaning?”

“Meaning I’m having a hard time seeing this as just another case to close.” He struggled to put what he was feeling into words. “I’m having a hard time seeing *you* as just another source in a case, instead of a beautiful woman sitting beside me in one of the most beautiful cities in the world."

He watched her face for her reaction, knowing he'd gone too far, but couldn't read her expression. Surprise? Interest? The bottom line, though, was that there were reasons for keeping his work and personal life separate, and he'd just crossed that line.

"I'm sorry—" he began.

"We're too different, you know." He couldn't tell if she was trying to convince him or herself. "You're an FBI agent. I'm a photographer and currently a student. You run on adrenaline, while I prefer my boring, ordinary life in the suburbs."

He swallowed hard. "Which is only one of many reasons why it wasn't appropriate for me to say what I did."

Kate shook her head, her smile still lingering. "Unless I'm feeling the same way."

Marcus hesitated before responding, aware of every reason why he should stop this conversation. They *were* too different. They lived in completely different worlds, and when this case was closed she'd walk out of his life. But he was also a man, and the way he felt wasn't because he felt sorry for her and her situation, or even him trying to step in and be the hero.

It was that something about her had drawn her to him. Her strength, her faith, her honesty . . . and that unexplainable, electrical feeling between them he couldn't ignore. Her face hovered in front of him, allowing him to breathe in the now-familiar citrusy scent of her perfume. Close enough for him to kiss her.

Ignoring the voice of reason in his head, he leaned in and brushed his lips across hers. Just for a moment. Just long enough for him to discover that he hadn't imagined the attraction between them.

Her phone rang beside her on the couch. She pulled away from him, then checked the caller ID.

"Bad timing, but it's my mom, hopefully with some good news."

"Wait . . ." He rested his hand over the phone. "Just so you know, I don't usually—okay, ever—kiss those I'm working with."

"And I don't usually—ever—kiss handsome FBI agents."

"So we're okay?"

She nodded, but the smile that had been playing on the edges of her lips disappeared as she answered the call. Marcus glanced at his watch and prayed for good news. Prayed that Rachel was finally awake. Because time for Sophie was running out and they needed answers.

ELEVEN

Kate stood up and walked back toward the window to take her mother's call while Marcus stepped into the small, adjacent kitchen to give her some privacy. "Mom . . . I was hoping you'd call. How's Rachel? Is she awake yet?"

Please, God. Please let Rachel be awake . . .

"Not yet. I'm sorry, Kate." There was tension in her mother's voice, along with fatigue. She knew her mother well. Knew that she'd be at that hospital at Rachel's side every moment possible, even it if meant not getting the rest she needed to keep going.

"How are you coping, Mom?" Kate tried to mask the disappointment in her voice.

"I'm tired, but okay. The women at church have been amazing. Always insisting I eat and get enough rest."

"And are you getting enough rest?" Kate asked, postponing the inevitable question about Rachel.

"Probably not, but the doctor gave me some sleeping pills that have helped. Eugenia makes sure I sleep at home at night and is even staying with me."

"I'm glad to hear that. You need your rest, and there isn't anything you can do for Rachel right now beyond being with her—and taking care of yourself."

Kate had talked to Eugenia, one of her mother's closest friends, before she left, asking if she would step in while she was gone and ensure her mother got enough rest. Thankfully, Eugenia had readily agreed.

"What about Sophie?" her mother asked. "Have you found out anything? Do you know who has her? The police have told me very little on this end."

It was the question Kate had been dreading to answer, as she'd yet to decide how much she should tell her mom. Did she share with her that her granddaughter was being held by people involved in diamond and weapons smuggling? That she was planning to make the exchange in less than forty-eight hours? And that if they didn't find the diamonds they might never see Sophie alive again?

She settled for leaving out the details for the moment, hoping her mother wouldn't press for answers until she had something positive to give her. Dealing with Rachel's injuries was enough on her mother's plate for the moment.

"There are still more questions than answers, Mom, but they are following every lead they have."

"I just don't understand, Kate. Tell me this doesn't have anything to do with Chad? He might not have ended up being the perfect husband, but I can't see him doing anything to harm Sophie or Rachel." Her mother paused to take a deep breath. "On the other hand, if this was just a random kidnapping . . . I think that's even more terrifying."

"Chad wasn't behind the kidnapping, but there is something you need to know, Mom." Kate stared at the apartments across the street with their colorful rows of flower boxes filled with hydrangeas, geraniums and roses. "I met with Chad this afternoon."

"You saw him?"

"I don't know how to tell you this, but he was hit by a truck after he left the church where we met."

"What? Is . . . is he okay?"

Kate paused, wishing she were there with her mother. Hating the fact that she was having to tell her this over the phone. "He didn't make it, Mom."

"No . . ." Her mom's voice caught. She was crying in the background. "How am I going to tell Rachel? Sophie and Chad . . . despite their marriage issues, they're her world."

"I don't know, Mom. All we can do is take it one day at a time." She needed to know more about Rachel. "What are the doctors saying about Rachel, Mom? How long until she wakes up?"

Kate waited for her mother's answer, needing

Rachel to be okay. Needing to be able to talk with her.

"I don't know. What I do know is that she's not doing well. That's the real reason I called, Kate. The doctors haven't said much, but I can tell they're worried. I can hear it in their voices. See it in their eyes. They've put her back on a breathing machine, and she's not responding the way she should. The doctors have decided to keep her in a medically induced coma for now."

Kate bit the side of her lip as a wave of nausea swept through her. That meant they were going to have to somehow find the diamonds without her sister's help.

God, we need Rachel to wake up. She is the only one who has answers that will help us get Sophie back.

"I want you to come home, Kate. It's not safe. The police implied to me that Chad *and* Rachel were involved in something illegal, but I can't believe that. Not about Rachel anyway. I don't know how to handle this."

"That's what I'm trying to find out, Mom. And please understand . . . as much as I want to be there with you right now." Kate fought the rising guilt for saying no, but there was no other option at the moment. Not if they wanted to get Sophie back alive. "I can't leave until I find Sophie. I'm working with the authorities here and staying at a safe house."

"I can't lose you both, Kate." Her mom sobbed. "You're all I have, you, Rachel and Sophie."

"Please don't cry. You're not going to lose me, Mom. I'm safe."

For now anyway.

"What do you know about him?" her mother asked. "This agent—Marcus—you told me about?"

"He's with the FBI, and he wants the same thing we do. He wants the men who hurt Rachel caught."

"Do you trust him?"

"Completely." She glanced over at him. He was talking to someone on his cell phone in the tiny kitchen. She trusted him because she had to trust someone. Trusted him because he'd never given her reason to not trust him.

"If you won't come home, then you must promise me you'll be careful, Kate. Promise me that. Please."

"You know I will, Mom. And I love you, Mom. You know that."

"I love you, too, Kate. Bring Sophie home as soon as you can."

Marcus hung up his cell phone in the small kitchen, then started pulling out plates and silverware for dinner while Kate spoke to her mother. He wished he could ignore the lingering feeling of her lips against his . . . and the light touch of her hand against his arm. Because she'd been right. They were too different, and he was fooling himself to think that whatever was happening between them could ever turn into a serious relationship beyond Paris.

But for some reason that knowledge hadn't been enough to stop him from kissing her. Which had him questioning his decisions. Relationships were complicated and messy, and ending up hurt wasn't a place where he wanted to go again. But on the other hand, Kate wasn't Nicole. And just because Nicole had hurt him, didn't mean there wasn't someone else out there who could love him wholly and unconditionally.

Someone like Kate.

Shoving his turbulent thoughts of Kate aside for the moment, he pulled out four plates and set them on the counter. Whatever feelings had passed between them were going to have to wait, because what mattered right now was getting the information they needed from Rachel. The clock was ticking, and they needed to know where the music boxes had been sent. Without Rachel, it was going to be a shot in the dark unless Kate was able to decipher her journal and figure out the truth.

As for the exchange, he planned to talk to Pierre and Jocelyn about their plan, but as far as he was concerned—assuming they had the diamonds by then—he didn't want Kate anywhere near it.

He pulled open the silverware drawer as Kate stepped into the kitchen. The smile she'd had earlier had vanished and her face had paled.

"Kate . . . what'd your mom say?"

"It's been rough."

"And your sister? Is she awake yet?"

Kate shook her head. "They've had to put her back on the ventilator. She's still in a coma."

"I'm so sorry."

"So am I. Because unless we find those diamonds . . ."

She didn't need to finish her sentence. They both knew what was at stake.

"If you don't mind, I need to freshen up a bit."

He caught the fatigue in her eyes and nodded, wishing he could make things right again for her.

Ten minutes later, Pierre and Jocelyn walked into the apartment with takeout for the four of them. The smell of garlic and spices permeated the apartment as they set the food onto the small dining room table. Kate had washed her face and freshened her makeup, but a hint of redness still registered in her eyes as she greeted them.

"Hope you both love Chinese," Pierre said.

"I didn't think I was hungry, but it does smell good," Kate offered.

"Not very Parisian, but I hope it will do. Beef with scallions and ginger, fried rice and cashew chicken." Jocelyn smoothed down her tan skirt, then started pulling the food out of the sacks.

"And, Kate, I don't know what to say about your brother-in-law, except I'm really, really sorry."

"Thank you, though I don't think the reality of the situation has completely sunk in yet," Kate said.

"They know they need to keep her alive and well if they want the diamonds," Pierre added.

"I hope, but I have so many questions. They already have Sophie. Why the need to grab me off the streets? It doesn't add up."

"We keep asking ourselves the same thing, because you're right. It doesn't add up," Jocelyn said. "What about your sister?"

Kate glanced at Marcus before answering. "I just got off the phone with my mother a few minutes ago. She's still unconscious."

"So we still don't have any idea where she sent the music boxes," Pierre said.

"Marcus thinks there might be a clue in her journal."

"It's worth a try."

"I have to try. She sent those diamonds to someone. If I want to get Sophie back, I need to find out who."

Marcus set the journals and albums onto the table beside the food. "I hate to make this a working dinner, but time isn't exactly on our side."

Kate started with the latest journal, turning pages between small bites of beef and fried rice. Journaling—along with her own version of shorthand—was a habit Rachel had picked up during high school.

"You can read that?" Marcus asked.

Kate held up her phone, where she'd looked up a cheat sheet to help decipher some of the phrases. "Enough to get the gist of most of it. We used to send notes to each other like this. It's a mixture of typical shorthand, using symbols and abbreviations for words and common phrases, along with our own 'language.' Rachel kept at it, though, and always used it when writing in her journals. It used to drive my mom crazy when she found one of our notes."

"You told me that she uses nicknames for everyone. Ace is the one I noticed a number of times from her time in Paris that you didn't know."

"I'll look for that name and see if I can put it in context."

She read through the pages, trying to sort through Rachel's shorthand, while the others looked through the photos. Setting aside the guilty feeling that came with it was proving to be impossible. A guilt over feeling as if she were trying to pry into her sister's private thoughts.

An hour later, Kate dropped the journal back onto the table, needing to take a break. Jocelyn and Pierre had already cleared away dinner, giving them more room to work on the small table.

"Anything?" Marcus asked.

Kate began flipping through the pages of one of the photo albums. "Nothing that seems to relate to what's happening now. Their marriage was clearly in trouble, but I don't think she knew anything about what Chad was involved in. In fact, she makes it very clear that she wanted to save their relationship. I know Rachel. If she knew what Chad was involved in and the danger it posed to her family, I think she'd have considered walking away before endangering Sophie's life."

Marcus tapped one of the photos of her and Rachel together. "Is that you and your sister?"

"Yes."

"You really do look a lot alike."

Kate took the album from him and smiled, feeling nostalgic over the shot. "I took her to the airport that day. She was on her way to Paris, hopeful she could work things out with Chad."

"Would you like some café?" Jocelyn asked, setting a tray of coffee cups and a pot onto the table. "It's decaf."

"I'd love some. Thank you," Kate said.

"I would, too," Marcus said. "Thank you, Jocelyn."

"What about Chad's relatives?" Pierre set down a plate with an assortment of petits fours from the bakery across the street and sat down. "Parents? Siblings? I know the police are still trying to contact his father, who lives here in Paris. His name is Andre Laurent."

"I don't know a lot about his family. Chad is—was—an only child. His mother died from breast cancer a few years back if I remember correctly," Kate said. While the fear still lingered, at least they were trying to find a solution. "His father came to their wedding in Dallas. He was a nice man, and he seemed happy to have Rachel as a part of his family."

"Have the police been able to speak with him yet?" Marcus asked, pouring himself a cup of coffee.

Pierre shook his head. "He's not picking up his cell phone, and he's not at his apartment."

"As soon as they find him, we need to question him," Marcus said.

"Here's another question." Kate took a sip of the coffee Marcus had poured her. "I think I understand how Chad stole the diamonds, but how was he intending to sell them without getting caught? You can't flood the market with diamonds without someone noticing."

"It's the same question every thief has to answer," Pierre said, eyeing the dessert tray, before picking up a small square piece of cake covered in pink fondant. "It seems like every few years or so someone tries to walk away with a fortune, but when they try to unload it . . . well, that's where they get caught."

"Pierre is right," Marcus said. "If it's a famous painting, for example, you can't exactly sell it on eBay. You have to sell it on the black market, where someone will hide it away among their private collection. And diamonds are the same. You can have them cut and polished, but flooding the market will ultimately raise questions."

"But isn't there a difference between breaking into a jewelry shop," Kate said, "and what Chad did? He might have been wrong, but he *assumed* no one knew what he was doing."

"True, but I'd think he'd still want to lay low," Jocelyn said. "If it were me, I'd have them cut and polished so there would be no way to trace them, but you'd still need to be careful. He wouldn't have wanted anyone to know—his bosses especially—what he was doing."

"So he was in no hurry to sell the diamonds," Kate said.

"Exactly. For the most part, thieves have two options. They can hide their spoils for months or even years, or the other option is to fence them."

"To whom?"

"He might have tried to cut a deal with an illegal wholesaler. Chad would sell the diamonds at a loss, but still make money, which in turn makes everyone happy."

"So that explains why he sent them to Rachel." Marcus picked a lemon tartlet from the tray and took a small bite. "He assumed they'd be safe there, and that Rachel would never discover she actually had the diamonds."

"What he didn't expect was that she would decide not to keep the music boxes," Kate said.

"And when someone discovered what he'd been doing and wanted the diamonds back . . . he had nothing to give them," Jocelyn said.

"So someone clearly knew what Chad was doing," Marcus threw out. "His boss? A coworker? Maybe whoever cut the diamonds for him?"

"His boss makes the most sense to me," Jocelyn said, picking up her second small piece of cake. This one was covered in bright lime-green fondant. "They would be the ones ultimately losing money from his buying and skimming."

"What about Rachel?" Pierre asked as he sat back in his chair, holding his coffee. "Is there a chance she found out what he was involved in? Or maybe was involved in it with him?"

The question stung even though it wasn't the first time the possibility had been brought up. But no matter how she looked at the situation, she couldn't bring herself to believe Rachel was involved.

"Like I said earlier," she said, "I couldn't find any mention of the diamonds in her journal—"

"That doesn't mean she didn't know what was going on," Pierre pressed.

Kate frowned at the implications.

"We have to look into everything, Kate," Marcus said, setting down his coffee.

"I know, it's just that . . . you don't know Rachel the way I do. She was horrible at keeping secrets. I can't see her sitting on a fortune and not breathing a word to anyone."

"But she knew something was off with her husband."

Kate closed her eyes for a moment. "She'd been distant the past few months, and I assumed it was because of the problems in her marriage. When Chad moved out of the house, she more or less became a single mom. It was hard for her."

Kate shook her head as snippets of their conversation the morning Rachel had been shot resurfaced. "The morning I found her—after she'd been shot—she told me that the last time she saw Chad, he was scared."

"About what?" Pierre asked.

"I don't know. She just said that the last time she went to see him in Paris, he'd told her he was scared. She'd hinted she was afraid he'd gotten himself involved in something illegal."

"Like smuggling diamonds. I'd lose sleep over getting caught, as well," Pierre said.

"She said he wouldn't tell her, but that it wasn't something she needed to worry about."

"What if they were in it together?" Jocelyn threw out. "What if she knew exactly what was in those music boxes because he told her? What if she was a part of the plan and they were waiting until they could sell the diamonds and buy an island or a house in Belize?"

Kate's head began to pound. "Then why not just keep the music boxes? I saw her mail those packages to someone."

"Maybe she wasn't returning them to him like you assumed, but hiding them so he wouldn't be able to find them," Pierre added.

"And betray Chad? No." While she couldn't believe Rachel had been involved in something illegal, neither could she believe she'd betray Chad.

Marcus reached out and squeezed her hand. "Unfortunately, we won't know for certain until she wakes up, so I think this is enough for now. Until we can speak with Rachel, everything we come up with is just speculation. What we need to focus on right now is simply finding those diamonds, and I think the place to start is Chad's father."

Kate nodded, grateful for his stepping in. He was right. Until Rachel woke up—if she woke up—he was right. They were simply grasping at straws.

"What else do you know about Chad's father?" Marcus asked.

"Like I said, I only met him twice. The first time was at Rachel and Chad's wedding. His English is pretty good so we chatted for a bit after the ceremony. He visited one other time in Dallas a few weeks after Sophie was born, but that was almost five years ago. I haven't seen him since."

Kate continued flipping through the photo albums, trying to remember what else she knew about the man. As with everything she did, Rachel had meticulously taken photos, labeled and organized them. Her last trip to Paris was no exception. Chad had taken some time off, but on days he had to work, Andre Laurent had taken her and Sophie around the city, but not to just the typical tourist destinations. Instead, he'd taken them to the Place des Vosges, the oldest square in Paris, where Victor Hugo had lived; the famous Berthillon ice cream shop for raspberry and mango ice cream; and one of the traditional, outdoor Le Guignol puppet shows for children.

She started to turn another page, then paused as the pieces of the puzzle began popping into place. "What if she sent the music boxes to Chad's father?"

"Why would she do that?" Jocelyn asked.

"I don't know, but the journal entries where she talks about Ace fit into the time period of this trip. Ace could be Chad's father. And look at this . . ."

"What is it?" Marcus asked.

"It's a photo of Chad's father from Rachel's last trip to Paris. They spent the morning at the Louvre.

I remember now that she told me that he is a copyist."

"A what?" Marcus asked.

"Haven't you ever visited a museum in Paris, Marcus?" Jocelyn asked.

Marcus frowned. "Of course."

"He goes to the Louvre every day and studies how to paint by actually copying the masterpieces." Kate nodded and handed him the photo. "He's especially interested in Renaissance artists."

"So what are you thinking?" Pierre asked. "That we might find him there?"

"It's worth a try," Kate said.

"The copyists arrive at 9:30 a.m., five days a week," Jocelyn explained. "And I suppose it's as good as any place to start looking for Monsieur Laurent if the police can't track him down sooner."

"And if we find him?" Kate asked.

"We?"

"I'm going with you, Marcus."

"Kate—"

"There is no way you can expect me to stay cooped up in this tiny apartment. Besides, if he knows something about the diamonds, do you think he'll just tell you or hand them over to you?"

"We've been over this before, Kate."

"She's right, Marcus." Jocelyn set her coffee cup on the table. "Kate's much more liable to get the truth out of him than you will be."

"Thanks, I thought you two were on my side. I can't take care of Kate and run this investigation."

"We'll be there as backup," Pierre said. "If they come after you, your job is to keep Kate safe, and we'll take them down."

Marcus shook his head, clearly not liking the idea.

"You know I need to be there," Kate started.

"No sneaking off and trying to do things on your own."

Kate nodded her head. "I promise."

"Then we'll need a layout of the museum and a detailed security plan," Marcus said, still not looking 100 percent convinced. "If we're going to do this, we're going to do it right."

TWELVE

"Kate . . . Kate?"

Kate's eyes flew open. She fought to suck in a breath of air. She sat up and felt the perspiration running down her forehead as she tried to figure out where she was.

"Kate, slow down." Marcus's voice tried to calm her. "You're okay. It was just a bad dream."

She looked up from the couch where she was sitting and tried to stop the room from spinning. Marcus knelt beside her, his hands gently on her shoulders.

"I thought I heard Sophie," she said. "She was calling me."

Marcus ran his hand down her arm. "It was just a dream, Kate."

She shook her head, still not convinced. Everything had seemed so real. She had heard Sophie's voice. She had to be somewhere nearby.

Marcus's expression softened. "You fell asleep after we all moved to the couch to finish talking about tomorrow. You looked so tired, though, I didn't want to wake you. I'm just waiting for Jocelyn. She had to run out for a few minutes. She's planning to stay with you. Remember?"

Kate nodded, then pressed her fingers against the sides of her temples as the room slowly began to come back into focus. They needed to find Chad's father. Planned to visit the Louvre in the morning. But she had been so tired. Thought she would just close her eyes for a few moments while the three of them finished planning.

"Sophie was there . . . hiding in the shadows, out of reach," she said, the dream still just as clear. "I wanted so bad to find her. To bring her home."

"I know. It was just a dream."

But it wasn't just a dream. Her heart was still pounding. Sophie was gone. That was real.

He ran his thumb down her cheek, the concern clear in his eyes. "Are you going to be okay?"

She grasped his hand and nodded. "I will be."

Eventually. Though she was quite certain that the scars left by this experience might never completely fade.

"Our conversation in the park was interrupted." He sat back, studying her. "You were going to tell me about your family."

She knew what he was doing. Trying to distract her. Trying to pull her away from the lingering panic of the dream.

"I . . . My parents had been married for twenty years when I was born. My sister was born eleven months later."

"That had to be a bit of an adjustment for them."

"It was." The grip of the dream began to diminish. "They were essentially starting parenthood in their mid-forties with two children under one. From the stories I've heard, it was quite a challenge. After twenty years of marriage, they had to completely rethink their entire lives. They owned a butchery, enjoyed traveling, and going out with friends, when all of a sudden they were taking care of children."

"So here's an odd question. Why didn't you or your sister decide to follow in your parents' footsteps and take over the butchery?"

Kate laughed, as the tension between them temporarily eased. "From around seventh grade through university, I was a vegetarian, something that horrified my father. I'm still not a big meat eater, though I don't mind a good, well-done steak every once in a while. They eventually sold the business and retired once we graduated from college."

"And Rachel? The two of you seem close."

Thoughts of her sister brought the dark shadow of the moment back over their conversation. "Rachel's had a few rough years. I'll admit I wasn't behind her relationship with Chad from the beginning, and now . . . well, I hate thinking that I was right about him."

"What had you concerned?"

She paused, wondering if he was asking as an agent or simply because he was trying to be supportive. "I'm not sure. He was good to her for the most part, but when he asked her to marry him they hardly knew each other. He'd traveled extensively. I think she suspected he was having an affair at one point. It wasn't something we spoke about. But the wonderful outcome of their relationship was Sophie. I love being an aunt, and have spoiled her from the day she was born."

"What about your father?"

"My father passed away five years ago."

"I'm sorry."

"I still miss him, but my mom's busy and doing well. Loves being a grandmother and takes care of Sophie several days a week." Kate stared across the room, ready to take the attention off herself. "What about you?"

"I have a big family," Marcus began. "Sort of a yours, mine and ours scenario."

"Really?"

"You sound surprised."

"I don't know. I kind of pictured you as an only child."

"And why is that?"

She leaned back slightly, taking the opportunity to study him. Blue eyes, hint of a five-o'clock shadow, determined chin and a strong jawline. "You seem more the strong, silent type. Independent. A deep need for privacy."

"I can assure you that growing up, I had no privacy. Actually there are seven of us and I'm the oldest. My parents divorced, then both of them remarried, so our family is a crazy mixture of half and step siblings."

"Are you close?"

"Work tends to get in the way, and we're spread out across the country, with my youngest brother in Korea, where he teaches English. I'm closest to one of my brothers, Shane. He lives on the other side of Dallas. I eat Sunday dinner with him and his family every month or two and go fishing and camping with them when I have time off. Hang out with his three boys."

He told her about his younger sister, who lived in Italy, the trip he took last year with his brothers to Chicago and about his faith that struggled during college until he'd determined to make it his own.

Though she was enjoying his stories, and the chance to see him as a person and not just an agent, she couldn't stifle a yawn.

"You're tired," he said.

She nodded. "I just need a good night's sleep."

Without any dreams.

"And tomorrow, if you—"

"I'll be fine tomorrow. Please . . . stop worrying."

"I can't make any promises, but I'll try." Marcus kissed her gently on the cheek then stood up as Jocelyn stepped through the front door. "I'll see you in the morning, then, Kate. Good night."

• • •

The next morning, Kate stayed close to Marcus as they made their way through the line of tourists across the open courtyard outside the Louvre's famed pyramid entrance, which provided light to the underground lobby. She knew Marcus still wasn't sold on the idea of her coming along, but at least he hadn't tried to make her stay behind. She watched the crowds for signs of the men who'd tried to snatch her, but so far she hadn't seen anyone who looked familiar.

Everywhere she looked, there were uniformed officers. She'd noticed them on the streets, in the metro and outside Notre Dame. Today, there seemed to be additional soldiers carrying automatic guns outside one of Paris's top tourist destinations.

"Is the police's presence always so . . . pronounced?" she asked, taking a step forward in the moving line.

"Eight-million-plus visitors come to the Louvre alone every year," Marcus told her. "Add a few networks of criminals, an influx of criminal gangs from Eastern Europe along with the occasional bomb threat, and I think the added security is probably here to stay. I've heard they've also increased the number of surveillance cameras and added a significant number of plainclothes officers."

"I guess I should feel safer."

But she didn't. Not really. Instead they seemed more a reminder of what could go wrong.

She walked through the security checkpoint, checked her bag through the X-ray machine, then studied the crowd while Marcus bought them two tickets. An older couple walked past, hand in hand, a young woman pushed a stroller, while a group of students armed with backpacks hurried to keep up with their teachers.

More reminders she wasn't here to enjoy the museum.

Because armed police, bomb threats, kidnappings and ransom notes weren't exactly a part of her day-to-day world. Her life ran on routine, made up of family, church and school. Until the past few days had managed to twist that life into something she couldn't even recognize.

She tried to stuff the fear away in a separate compartment—one she'd have to deal with when this was all over. For now, they needed to go ahead with their plan because so far the police hadn't been able to locate Chad's father. Without Rachel—and without Monsieur Laurent—their chances of finding the diamonds were diminishing by the hour. And the clock was ticking.

"I guess you've never had the chance to visit the Louvre?" Marcus asked, pulling her away from her thoughts.

"No." The desire to forget reality and simply meander through the thousands of treasures tucked away throughout the famed museum tugged harder.

"Originally," Marcus began, "it was built as a fortress back in the twelfth century, but several hundred years later it was reconstructed to serve as a royal palace."

Kate glanced at the brochure he'd handed her, the tension in her gut refusing to lift.

"By the end of the eighteenth century," he continued, "the Louvre had become an art museum, filled with royal artifacts as well as acquisitions from conquered lands, which is why you'll find almost everything you could imagine. Egyptian antiques, ancient Greek and Roman crown jewels—"

"And my favorite." She flashed him a weak smile. "The *Mona Lisa*."

"And that of half the people in this museum at the moment."

But today she wasn't expecting to catch a glimpse of Leonardo da Vinci's masterpiece, or the armless beauty of the *Venus de Milo* or any of the other famed offerings of the museum. Today she was simply praying to find answers that would lead her to her niece.

Using the museum's official map, Marcus led her through a maze of halls and rooms. Throughout, painters were working on creating their own replicas of some of the most famous works of art in the world. With their easels and stools set up across the diverse rooms of the Louvre's galleries, in front of the gold-framed works of art displayed on colored walls.

"Do you see him in here?" Marcus asked.

"Not yet."

She kept walking beside Marcus, barely glancing at the art they passed. Her nerves were on edge as she searched the crowd for Monsieur Laurent. For the men who were after her.

A moment later, she found him. Andre Laurent was standing inside the grand Renaissance room, a fine paintbrush in his hand next to a colorful palette of paints. She crossed the large room, stopping half a dozen feet from where he stood, staring at the painting hanging on the wall in front of him. He wore a collared shirt and a striped vest, as well as the same overgrown mustache she remembered. Sophie had once commented how he always tickled her cheek when he greeted her.

"*Excusez-moi*, *Monsieur Laurent* . . ."

Andre Laurent looked away from the painting to Kate. The older man's brow furrowed for a moment as if trying to remember who she was, then shifted into a broad smile. "You're Rachel's sister."

"Yes. I'm Kate." She smiled at the older man. "I'm visiting Paris for a few days. Rachel told me you spend most of your time here. I was hoping to find you."

He set down his paintbrush and paints, then shook his head, still clearly surprised. "It's good to see you." He smiled, then kissed her lightly on each cheek before pulling back and catching her gaze. "You look beautiful, Kate, and so much like Rachel. The same eyes and cheekbones."

"Thank you. And your painting. It's beautiful, as well."

"The artist is Bernardino Luini, and he painted this almost five hundred years ago." He pointed to the painting on the wall. "*Nativity and Annunciation to the Shepherds.* Five hundred years ago, and I'm still learning from him."

"Rachel told me how much you enjoyed creating replicas."

"Four hours a day. Five days a week. Each canvas must be a different size from the original and signed, dated and stamped. There are one hundred fifty of us who waited a year to get this privilege. For these few hours I'm here every day it's like I become the student to the master painter, and the Louvre is the book from which I learn to read. That was first said by the renowned Postimpressionist painter Paul Cezanne, who did the same thing over one hundred fifty years ago. But enough of me, I had no idea you were in Paris. Rachel didn't tell me. How long has it been . . . five years?"

"Yes. It's been a long time. When Sophie was born." Kate turned to Marcus, unable to put off the inevitable. “I’d like you to meet Marcus O’Brian. He’s an FBI agent from the United States.”

M. Laurent shook Marcus’s hand. “FBI? I’m afraid I don’t understand. I assumed you were in Paris on holiday.”

“No, we’re here to speak to you about Chad.”

M. Laurent’s face paled. “I’m sorry . . . I don’t understand.”

Kate glanced around the room, where half a dozen tourists studied the paintings in the room. “Is there somewhere private we could go? The police have been trying to find you.”

The older man clasped his hands together. “Chad told me to be careful. Told me to go to a hotel for a few days. That he was in some kind of trouble, but he wouldn’t tell me what was going on.”

“M. Laurent, I don’t know how to tell you this, but—”

He looked up and caught her gaze. “He’s dead, isn’t he?”

Kate drew in a deep breath and nodded. “I’m so sorry. He was hit by a truck yesterday afternoon near Notre Dame. I know that he and my sister had their issues, but he was still family. I really am so, so sorry.”

M. Laurent stumbled backward a step, then sat down on his stool. “I knew something was wrong, but he wouldn’t tell me. I even tried to call Rachel to see what she knew, but I never was able to get through."

"Chad *was* involved with some dangerous people," Marcus added. "We're still not one hundred percent sure if they were the cause of his death, but Kate is helping me find answers."

"What about Rachel?" the older man asked.

Kate's stomach felt queasy at the question. She hadn't expected to have to tell him about Rachel and Sophie, as well. "Chad didn't tell you?"

"Tell me what? Except for his call on Tuesday, telling me to go to a hotel, it's been at least a month since I spoke to Chad."

"She . . ." Kate looked to Marcus, then told M. Laurent briefly what had happened with Rachel. "She's still in the hospital, and will more than likely be there for a while."

"Did this have anything to do with whatever Chad was involved in?"

"Yes. They are looking for something that he had and believe Rachel now has."

"What about Sophie?"

"They kidnapped her. As leverage."

"Took her?"

"The people who shot Rachel. There's evidence they brought her to Paris. Which is why I'm here."

M. Laurent tugged on the side of his mustache. "Rachel's such a sweet girl. And that Sophie. When they were here in Paris I enjoyed showing them around the city. Made an old man's heart feel proud, and young again, for that matter. Never did understand my son's foolish actions. She's so good at keeping in touch. Sends me photos of her and Sophie at least once a month, along with birthday and Christmas letters. Chad was really my only family except for Rachel and Sophie, and now . . . She promised to come back and visit as soon as she could."

"And I'm certain she still will. She loved her time in Paris."

M. Laurent shook his head. "I'm sorry. This is all so very . . . confusing to me."

Kate waited while a group of schoolchildren followed their teachers through the room, barely paying attention to the masterpieces surrounding them.

"M. Laurent," Kate finally said, "I understand that this is difficult for you, but in order to get Sophie back, we need certain information. Marcus would like to ask you a few questions."

"Of course. Let me pack up my paints and turn them in first. I can't paint any more today anyway." He quickly organized his things, allowing Kate and Marcus to help carry his easel and stool to where the copyists stored their supplies. "I'm not sure how I can help, though. Like I said, Chad didn't tell me anything."

"Can you tell me how Chad sounded the last time you spoke to him, M. Laurent?" Marcus asked as they started for the exit of the room, the stunning works of art surrounding them momentarily forgotten.

"It was clear something was wrong," he said. "I tried to get Chad to talk, because I knew he was involved in something he shouldn't be. He seemed nervous. Distracted. Like there was a ghost behind every shadow. He thought he could continue doing whatever it was he was doing without getting caught. And now . . . now my son is dead and his family torn apart because of stupid decisions he made."

"There were some music boxes Chad bought for Sophie," Marcus continued as they walked into the next room. "He sent them to her for her birthday and Christmas the past couple years. Rachel shipped them to someone. We think it might have been you."

His weathered hand clasped Kate's arm. "Rachel did send them to me. They were beautiful. Made in Switzerland, and they weren't cheap."

"Do you still have them?"

"I couldn't bring myself to sell them. For one, they were beautiful. I know Rachel worries about me. I have some health problems and can't work the way I used to. She thought I could use the money. I thought maybe there would come a time when she would take them back."

Kate looked to Marcus. "Would it be possible for us to see them?"

"Of course. They're at my apartment. But there is something else you need to know."

"What is that?"

M. Laurent stopped. "Chad gave me an envelope a few weeks ago. He told me if anything happened to him, I needed to open it."

"Do you still have that envelope, M. Laurent?" Marcus asked.

"Yes, but I just . . . I never expected to have to open it."

Kate felt a shiver of fear creep up her spine, praying that whatever Chad had wanted to tell his father from beyond the grave would help them save Sophie.

THIRTEEN

Marcus stepped into the elevator behind Kate and M. Laurent as the older man pushed the button for the fifth floor of his apartment building. After two days in Paris he already missed his roomy town house and decent-sized yard in Dallas. Growing up in West Texas had given him a love—and need—for space. But space was a luxury in this city.

"How long have you lived in this building, M. Laurent?" Kate asked.

"Moved here with my wife, Monique, three decades ago. Chad was about . . . seven, I think. The building had a face-lift a decade ago in an attempt to erase the signs of pollution. It boasts of a musty cellar and no parking space, but my wife saw charm with the wooden floors and fireplaces. She fell in love with the place the first time we set foot in it. And she loved it until the day she died."

"I'm sorry for your losses," Kate said. "I know this has to be extremely difficult for you."

M. Laurent pulled a set of keys from his pocket. "Honestly, I'm just glad Monique isn't here to have to go through this. I'm not sure how she would have dealt with losing Chad this way. He was her world."

The elevator stopped, and the doors opened. They stepped into the small landing, where an overhead light turned on automatically. A musty smell filled the air, along with the hint of men's cologne. Marcus stepped across the space, wishing he could shake the uneasy feeling that had settled in the pit of his stomach.

So far the men they were after had managed to stay one step ahead of them. He was tired of losing. Tired of surprises. He needed answers—needed those diamonds—and prayed that they'd finally come to the right place.

Marcus turned to Kate, wishing—not for the first time—that he had his weapon. "I'd like to go inside first, M. Laurent, if you don't mind."

The older man hesitated in front of the door. "You think they might be after me?"

"Chad was clearly worried about you, and I don't want to take any chances."

The older man shook his head then fumbled to unlock the door. "I thought Chad had more common sense than to get involved in some devilish scheme that would end up getting him killed."

Marcus stepped into the apartment ahead of them both, then stopped short on the threshold. Like Rachel's house, it appeared as if every square inch of the tiny apartment had been gone through. Drawers had been dumped out, couch cushions strewn across the floor and artwork torn down from the wall.

Marcus hesitated, a sick feeling spreading through him. "M. Laurent . . ."

"What is wrong?" M. Laurent froze in the doorway. "You were right."

"Marcus . . . what is it?" Kate stepped into the apartment beside Chad's father.

M. Laurent's face paled. "They've been here."

"M. Laurent," Marcus said, "call the police on your cell phone. Kate, stay here with him while I search the apartment to ensure the intruder isn't still here."

The older man nodded as he pulled his phone out of his pocket. "There are two rooms down the hall to the left with a couple large closets. The kitchen is to the right."

Marcus caught Kate's gaze, and hesitated. "You okay?"

She nodded, but he caught the fear in her eyes and guessed what she was thinking. Things like this didn't happen in the Dallas suburbs. She lived an ordinary life, where the only crimes that touched her were the ones she read about online or saw on the nightly news on the television. But now everything had changed.

Kate watched Marcus methodically search the living room with its large bay window and access to a small balcony, before heading down the hall to the bedrooms while M. Laurent spoke to the police on his cell. How had they gotten to this point? They hadn't mentioned the diamonds yet to Chad's father, but whoever was after them clearly thought the older man was somehow involved. Or thought he had what they were looking for.

She tried not to panic as she sent up another prayer for protection. She was worrying too much. Marcus was a seasoned agent who knew how to handle a situation like this. And besides, more than likely whoever had trashed the place had already left.

Kate heard the soft creak of footsteps behind her a moment before he grabbed her. Instinct kicked in. She screamed, then automatically jammed her elbows into her attacker's rib cage. He tightened his grip around her with one arm, then covered her mouth with his hand. Chad's father lunged toward him and tried to pull her away, but the assailant shoved M. Laurent backward with his foot, slamming the older man into the wall.

Kate glanced down at the man's sleeve tattoos and fought harder. Her heart raced faster. Bile filled her throat.

He'd found her.

She bit hard across the palm of his hand, then screamed again, but the pain didn't stop her attacker from dragging her toward the narrow, spiraling staircase that led to the small lobby of the building.

Her eyes widened in panic as Marcus stepped into the landing, running toward her when he realized what was happening. "Let her go."

"Don't even try to follow." Her attacker held up a gun Kate hadn't noticed in the commotion. "Either of you."

Marcus hesitated as M. Laurent stumbled to his feet, a thin stream of blood trickling down his head where he'd hit the wall.

"Are you okay, M. Laurent?" Marcus asked, his eyes never leaving Kate.

"I think so."

Kate felt the man's gun press against the side of her head. She struggled for air. Struggled against the fear. "Marcus, don't let him take me. Please."

"Put the gun down," Marcus said. "You don't want to do this."

The man laughed. "I'm not here to play games or negotiate. And I will kill her if I have to. I only want one thing. The diamonds she has."

"What diamonds?" M. Laurent asked, still looking dazed.

"I guess your son didn't tell you about them," her attacker said.

"They're in the music boxes," Kate blurted.

"Nice try, but I found the music boxes in the apartment, and they're empty. Chad tried to play games as well, but no more."

The last flicker of hope left Kate. If he was telling the truth and the diamonds weren't here, someone got to them before they did. And they now had no idea where they were.

"She takes me to the diamonds, and she lives . . . maybe."

"You already have Sophie," Kate said, trying to take out the desperation in her voice. "Tell me where she is."

He didn't answer as Kate stumbled down the narrow staircase, a step in front of her attacker, trying not to trip. The paint was peeling on the walls. The staircase clearly hadn't been a part of the renovations over the past few years. Sirens screamed in the background as he pulled open the door to the small lobby filled with nothing more than a mailbox on one side stuffed with flyers. She started to pull away from him, but he jammed his elbow into her rib cage. Kate gasped for breath as the pain ripped through her side, and she stumbled backward.

Marcus was forming his plan before the door to the stairwell closed. There were three ways down to the lobby. The stairs, the elevator and a service elevator used to move furniture and other large belongings. He opted for the stairs.

"Wait here for the police," he told M. Laurent.

The old man nodded.

His mind shifted through the facts as he took

the stairs two at a time. He'd seen the music boxes smashed into pieces on the floor of the back room of M. Laurent's apartment. And no sign of the diamonds. Which meant they still didn't have the leverage they needed. But neither was he going to let the man take Kate. Career had always managed to trump relationships. He hadn't had time. Hadn't wanted to take the time. Kate had changed all of that, and he had no plans of losing her.

At the bottom of the staircase, Marcus eased open the door to the lobby. Kate's kidnapper had just stepped out of the lobby with Kate, as an older woman walked in, carrying a bag of groceries. Her kidnapper slipped the gun behind him, clearly not wanting to make a scene.

Kate took advantage of his hesitation. She jammed her elbow into his ribs, grabbed the bag of groceries from the woman and slammed them against her attacker's head, throwing him off balance.

Marcus lunged toward him, shoving him outside the lobby and pushing him against the sidewalk facedown. The struggle was over in a matter of seconds. The other man tried to fight him, but Marcus pinned his arms behind him and held him down.

"Not so fast," he said in French, while Kate kicked away the gun that had fallen onto the sidewalk in the scuffle.

"You're foolish," the man said. "The people I work for want those diamonds. And they're not people you want to mess with."

"Who are you working for?" Marcus asked.

The bald man spat on the ground then turned his head.

Keeping a tight grip on the man, Marcus looked up at the older woman, who had backed up against the lobby door, jaw slack, her groceries strewn across the front walk.

"Are you okay, ma'am?" he asked in French.

She nodded, clearly shaken.

"If you tell the manager what you lost, I'll make sure everything is replaced. In the meantime, I suggest you return to your apartment. The police will want to speak to you later."

The matronly woman nodded again, eyes wide, then without a word headed up the stairs.

"What about you, Kate?"

Kate nodded, her chest heaving as she fought to catch her breath. "I just want this to be over."

"It will be. Soon."

Which was what he wanted to believe, but he wasn't sure it was going to be that easy. They still had to find the diamonds. And Sophie.

Sirens blared louder as two police vehicles pulled up at the street and officers exited, weapons drawn on the three of them.

Marcus held up one hand, still pinning the man down with his knee as he spoke to the officers in French. “My name is Marcus O’Brian. I’m an agent with the FBI working with French intelligence. This man is wanted in connection to weapons and diamond smuggling, as well as attempted kidnapping.”

“Don’t move.” The two officers walked toward them.

“You can confirm my story with Pierre Durand, who works with French intelligence,” Marcus continued.

One of the officers turned away to speak on his radio for a minute then turned back to Marcus. “Your identification?”

Marcus tossed him his credentials.

“You check out, but we’ll still need your statement.”

“Of course.” Marcus looked to Kate, then turned back to the officers. “Can you make sure this man is booked? I’ll be down there as soon as I can.”

“Certainly, monsieur.”

Marcus nodded. “*Merci.*”

A moment later, Kate’s attacker was handcuffed and loaded into the police vehicle.

Marcus let out a sigh of relief, then turned his attention to Kate. “You did well. I’m impressed with how you kept your head.”

Kate leaned back against the outside wall of the lobby. “Thanks, but my head is pounding. I’m shaking like a leaf, and I’m not sure I’m going to be able to keep my breakfast down."

"Bend over and put your head between your legs." He rested his hands on her shoulders. "Breathe slowly. It's over. He can't hurt you anymore."

Her breathing had slowed down and the color began to come back to her cheeks.

She started to stand up again.

"Slowly, Kate. Slowly."

Marcus pulled her against his chest, and held her tightly against him, giving her time to find her equilibrium.

"He said the diamonds weren't there," she said, looking up at him.

"I know. I saw the music boxes, Kate. They were smashed. And empty. There were no signs of the diamonds."

"I don't understand what Chad was trying to do. Where are the diamonds? And why do they think I have them?"

"I don't know."

"What do we do now?" she asked, pressing her hands against his chest.

He wished he could whisk her away from all of this, but this wasn't going to be over until the diamonds were found and whoever was behind this was put behind bars.

"First I want to check on M. Laurent, then I'm planning to head to the police station. I have a few questions to ask our intruder."

"Sounds like a pretty safe place at the moment."

"Yes, though I still haven't decided what to do with you." Though at the moment, as she looked up at him with those wide eyes, kissing her came to mind. He filed away the thought for later when he had the chance to do so properly.

"He clearly isn't the only person involved," Marcus continued. "But if we're lucky, he'll lead us to the others behind this."

"What if we're actually looking at two separate groups who know about and are after the diamonds?" Kate asked.

Marcus mulled over her question. "It makes sense, actually. Sophie is kidnapped by one, and the other somehow thinks you—or Rachel—has the diamonds."

"And it would explain why someone is after me. Because whoever has Sophie already has all the leverage they need. There's no need for them to take me, as well."

"It's a theory worth looking into. For now, we need to check on M. Laurent and ask the man a few questions. Because something tells me he knows more than he's been willing to share."

Marcus punched number five on the elevator, his hand tight around Kate's. All he could think about was that Kate was safe. And that he was going to make sure she stayed that way. "By the way, that was quite a stunt you pulled down there. You completely took him by surprise."

"I've been taking a self-defense class back in Dallas. Never thought I'd use what I've learned, though. Realized, as well, that it's one thing to practice self-defense in a classroom, and another to put it into practice in a real scenario. When someone looks you in the eye with the intent of hurting you . . . I'm not sure anything can completely prepare you for that."

"What motivated you to take the class?" he asked.

"While I was in Africa, a friend of mine ran into some problems with poachers while we were filming. Long story short, she was kidnapped by poachers who were tied to an international crime syndicate."

"Wow. Apparently there are a few things about you I don't know." He turned to her as the elevator doors opened and winked at her. "I'm wondering what else I don't know about you, Kate Elliot."

On the fifth floor, the door to the Laurent apartment was open. Chad's father sat on the couch, staring out the window, his hands clutching a large envelope.

"M. Laurent?" Kate quickly went into the kitchen, returning with a wet rag, and began wiping the blood from the older man's head that had now dried across his temple and down his cheek. "It's just a small cut. Head wounds always look worse than they are."

"I thought you . . ." He looked at her, confused.

"The police have taken the man into custody, M. Laurent," Marcus said. "Kate's got quite a left swing."

M. Laurent looked around the room and shook his head, looking defeated. "They took my son. My granddaughter. What else do they want from me?"

"I don't know, but we will find out," Kate said. "We're going to get some answers from the man."

"But I need some answers from you first, M. Laurent." Marcus sat down on the cushioned chair across from the couch. "What do you know about the diamonds?"

M. Laurent leaned forward. "I know where they are."

Kate looked to Marcus, then back to Chad's father. "You know where the diamonds are?"

"You have to understand, when you showed up at the museum . . . I didn't know if I could trust you. And then when that man showed up, everything happened so fast. I've just lost my son. Found out my granddaughter was taken. I wasn't—I'm not—thinking straight."

"But Marcus said the music boxes in your apartment were empty," Kate said.

"They are. Now. When I first received the music boxes, I didn't know who they were from, though I suspected Chad, not Rachel. I knew he was hiding something. Thought he might be in trouble. One night I was listening to one of them, and I realized that they would make the perfect hiding place."

"And you opened them up."

M. Laurent nodded. "I took the first one apart, and inside . . . I couldn't believe it. There was a small sack of raw, uncut diamonds. The only thing I know about diamonds is what I've learned from Chad over the years. Which meant I knew they were worth a fortune, but also that in the state they were in, they could be traced."

"Why didn't you go to Chad?"

"I think I was afraid to find out the truth. Afraid to discover that my son was involved in something illegal. At the same time I'd been working to track where the package had come from and found out Rachel had sent them."

"Do you think she knew about the diamonds?"

M. Laurent shook his head. "I called her and asked her why she'd sent the boxes. She told me she felt like Chad was trying to buy Sophie's love. Thought I would appreciate them. I'm certain she didn't know about the diamonds, though, and I didn't tell her."

"Where are the diamonds, M. Laurent?" Marcus asked.

He clutched the envelope tighter, creasing its edges. "After I found them in the first music box, I opened up the rest of the music boxes and knew

I needed a place to hide them. They weighed around three and a half kilograms . . . almost eight pounds."

"Five million dollars' worth."

"You can see why I was afraid. I decided to hide them in plain sight. At the Louvre."

"At the Louvre? Where?" Kate asked.

"It seemed perfect." M. Laurent stared at the throw rug in the center of the living room as he spoke. "There are a number of regulations for anyone who wants to be a copyist at the Louvre. Most of the rules are to stop someone from trying to make a copy they could in turn sell as authentic. Your work has to be a different size from the original, you can't reproduce the signature of the artist and you can only bring into the museum canvas or drawing paper that is authorized. And as you saw, we keep our canvases and supplies in storage at the Louvre. I found a way to hide them, among the brushes and paint."

"So the diamonds were there with you every day."

"It was a temporary solution only, and one I was planning to talk to Chad about. Now that will never happen because he . . . he never listened. All the diamonds in the world aren't worth my son's life." He looked up and caught Kate's gaze. "Whoever has Sophie wants the diamonds, don't they?"

Kate nodded. “The exchange is in less than twenty-four hours now.”

“I’ll get you the diamonds, and . . .” M. Laurent handed Marcus the envelope he was holding. “This was what he gave me in case something happened to him. It didn’t save my son, but maybe it will help save Sophie and put an end to all of this.”

Kate watched Marcus slide out the contents of the envelope onto the coffee table in the middle of the living room. “What is all of this?”

Marcus started flipping through the papers. “Chad must have known he was about to get caught. It looks like names, dates, contacts . . .”

Chad’s father shook his head. “What was he thinking?”

“Most people get involved in something like this with the strong belief they won’t get caught,” Marcus said. “I’m sure your son was no different.”

M. Laurent shook his head sadly. “And those diamonds? They were worth what? The life of my son? Of my daughter-in-law and granddaughter?”

“I’m sorry, M. Laurent.” Marcus placed the papers back in the envelope and stood up.

“What next?” the older man asked.

“We need to go get the diamonds. And pray we now have the leverage we need to save Sophie’s life.”

FOURTEEN

Kate sat on the stern of the boat beside Marcus in one of the bright orange seats, telling herself to relax. She'd agreed to join him for one of the legendary Bateaux-Mouche cruises. He'd called it a well-needed distraction, because there was nothing they could do until tomorrow.

She, on the other hand, called *him* a distraction. He'd changed into a pair of black jeans and a collared green shirt for their trip down the Seine. Which meant she hadn't failed to notice how handsome he was with his tanned skin, dark hair, bright eyes and that touch of five-o'clock shadow. Or how he stirred something inside of her she hadn't felt for a long time. And while those feelings scared her, her heart was trying to convince her that Marcus was different.

Kevin's walking out on her had taught her a lot. She'd learned that self-worth could never come from a man. Learned that trying to change a man would never happen. Learned that her relationship with God had to be a priority. And learned that the kind of man she wanted to be with one day was a man who was honest, strong, had a deep faith and was comfortable with himself.

Like Marcus.

Which was exactly why she should have turned

down his offer. Because as much as she wanted to be here, with him, she hadn't come to Paris to fall in love. Even now that they'd found the diamonds, there were still too many questions that needed to be answered. Marcus and Pierre had questioned the man who'd attacked her. They'd learned his name was Davin Bernard, and he had former convictions for theft and possession of stolen property. But so far, the man who'd tried to grab her was refusing to talk.

The envelope Chad had left with his father had given them a significant amount of evidence they needed to build on Marcus's case, but it was going to take time to sort through everything. Marcus had spent hours going through the files at the safe house until Pierre had convinced him to stop for the night. Everything was set for tomorrow's exchange, which meant for the moment, the best thing they could all do was get some rest.

Kate gazed out across the Seine as they glided under one of the lit bridges, trying to let go of the fear and worry for the moment. The sun had set thirty minutes ago, and now, the lights from the city and the bridges were reflecting against the river, creating the backdrop just as she'd expected. Romance, history and timeless beauty all enveloped the views surrounding them.

Maybe Marcus had been right. Maybe the distraction was exactly what she needed.

"Penny for your thoughts?" he asked, nudging her with his elbow.

She looked up at him and shot him a smile. "I'm sorry."

"I have a feeling you haven't heard a word I've been saying."

She searched her memory. The last thing she remembered he'd been telling her about Pont-Neuf, the oldest remaining bridge in Paris, that had been depicted in one of Renoir's paintings. "This was a good idea, but I'm clearly not the greatest company tonight."

"I didn't ask you to come and entertain me. I asked you to join me because I enjoy being with you. And we both needed a break and some fresh air."

The familiar uneasiness crept in around her. She knew he'd taken every precaution to keep her safe, but even she knew he couldn't control everything. The boat was filled with tourists with cameras, and an energetic young woman gave a live commentary on the lit-up sights along the banks of the river.

"They're not here, Kate. You're on a slow-moving boat along the Seine, in the most romantic city in the world with a fairly good-looking guy—if I say so myself—who thinks you look beautiful tonight."

She felt her cheeks blush at the compliment and couldn't help but laugh. "You're right. About the romantic city and the fairly good-looking guy, anyway."

He grabbed her hand and squeezed her fingers. "I'm going to do everything I can to keep you safe. I promise."

She shook her head. "Don't promise me that. Rachel thought she could keep Sophie safe, but she couldn't. I've realized that as much as I hate it, there are simply some things I can't do. She's my little sister. I should have been there to protect her, but I wasn't."

"None of this is your fault, Kate."

"Deep down inside, I know that, but even so it's hard to separate the frustration and the fear from the guilt."

"Try to forget everything else for the moment. You told me you'd always longed to visit Paris. The situation with your niece and sister aside, what are your impressions?"

He was trying to distract her again, and she appreciated it. She'd spent the past two days thinking about tomorrow's exchange. He'd tried—more than once—to convince her to let someone else take her place. But she couldn't—wouldn't—take any chances with her niece's life. Which meant tomorrow, she was going to have to trust him with her life.

But he was right. She needed to let go what she couldn't control, even if it was only temporary.

"Maybe I'm just a crazy romantic, but Paris is

more beautiful than I imagined, if that's possible." She let out a soft sigh. The city was lit up as they'd passed the Place de la Concorde, and then the Musée d'Orsay before looping around Notre Dame and heading back toward the Eiffel Tower.

"When I was nine, I had a poster of Paris on my wall. I loved the movie *Sabrina*, and was determined to learn French." She chuckled at the memories. "I think my parents agreed that I was crazy. Up to that point, Paris, Texas, was about as far away from home as I'd ever been."

Marcus's smile widened as he listened to her.

She shook her head. "It sounds silly now. It's just one of dozens of cities with centuries of history and culture, but somehow Paris was the city that captivated me."

"I know my sister, Macy, wouldn't say it's just a city. Her dream as a teenager was to visit Rome. To this day, she admits she's not sure what it was, but she ended up marrying an Italian."

"Ah . . . those Italian men. They'll get you every time."

Marcus laughed. "She's still completely enchanted by everything Italian."

"I think my obsession, if you want to call it that, began as simply the desire to see the world beyond my small town that included the local grocery store, a gas station and post office."

"You have traveled, though."

Kate breathed in a calming breath. "Last year in Africa working on the documentary. Before that I took several mission trips with my church to Haiti and one to Mexico. I'm determined to travel more, though."

"So Paris has lived up to your expectations?"

"Yes . . . and no. On one hand, it's beautiful and romantic, and exactly how I imagined it would be. But it's hard for me to see the city without remembering the real reason I'm here."

She wasn't ready to mention the other memories that fought to surface, as well. The fact that she'd planned to come here on her honeymoon with Kevin.

"I've tried to play the role of tour guide a bit. Has it helped some?"

She laughed. "And you've been perfect, though you are missing the French accent. Texas drawl doesn't quite cut it here."

Marcus's smile broadened as he settled back in his chair, his hand still firmly grasping hers. "I know these aren't the circumstances you dreamed of seeing this city in, but for me . . . tonight . . . everything *is* perfect."

His words seemed to hover between them like the kissed they'd shared. She wanted to ask him what he wanted to happen between them when all of this was over. If something more was even a possibility. But for the moment, she simply wanted to embrace this moment and get to know him better.

"What about you?" she asked. "How much have you traveled?"

"This isn't the first time I've traveled for work, and I also traveled a lot growing up. My father was in the air force and we were posted several times overseas."

"Thus the French?"

"Partly. I spent two years in a university exchange program in France. It was after that I decided that I wanted to follow in my father's footsteps. I joined the military, but eventually went to work for the FBI."

"Any regrets?"

"None, though according to some of my siblings, friends and my mom, I'm too busy and too driven. It's a combination that tends to sour relationships . . . Well, we probably shouldn't even go there."

"You wouldn't be the first one with a soured relationship in their past." Kate laughed, feeling herself relax for the first time all evening. Tomorrow would still come, and it was going to have enough worries of its own.

"Can I ask another question, then?"

"Okay."

"It's personal." He hesitated, as if giving her a chance to change her mind.

She watched a couple having their photo

taken. Honeymooners? An anniversary? She still imagined being in love one day with the right person—and visiting Paris together.

She let her gaze sweep Marcus's face. In the short time she'd known him, she'd been forced to trust him, and he'd been trustworthy. Somehow, they'd managed to move past the layer of superficiality, which both thrilled and terrified her at the same time. Because while it might simply be the lights, the music playing in the background and the city itself, right here with him was where she wanted to be at the moment.

"It's okay," she said.

"There's a sadness behind your eyes when you talk about love and relationships. Almost a longing. Like you lost someone you love."

She nodded, amazed at how perceptive he was. She'd seen two sides of him. The take-charge, reel-'em-in and take-'em-down side. And the other, softer side that made her know he saw her as a person and not just another case.

"His name was Kevin. He was funny, good-looking, and at the time, I thought he was everything I'd been looking for." She paused, unsure of how much she wanted to share. "We dated for six months, and when he asked me to marry him, I was over the moon. We planned to take a European cruise for our honeymoon. France, Italy and England . . . I thought our relationship was perfect. Turned out, he didn't."

"What happened?"

Kate stared out at the water. "He eloped with my best friend and maid of honor. Left me a Dear Jane letter."

"Ouch," he said. "That had to have hurt."

She waited for the pain and humiliation of the moment to rewash over her, but it didn't. Instead, she saw the man sitting next to her. No pity. No judging. Just a genuine concern for what it must have been like for her.

"It was humiliating, actually, and I've pretty much tried to avoid men ever since. Unfortunately, my mother and my sister have been convinced that setting me up with someone would make me forget about Kevin." She shifted slightly in her seat. "What about you? Who's the girl who broke your heart?"

Marcus's brow rose slightly at her question. "And I thought I was the perceptive one."

Kate shot him a smile. "Who says you need interrogating skills to be perceptive?"

"Touché. Her name was Nicole. She was a ballet dancer. Beautiful and exotic. We'd been dating a few months when she showed up at my apartment one night and gave me an ultimatum. It was my job or her."

"Ouch. What did she want you to do? Quit?"

"I suppose. But for me, I was hit with the realization that no matter how much energy I put into our relationship, it wasn't going to work out between us. I think I'd kept forcing things, trying to make things work. Turned out my job was just one piece of the puzzle. We lived different lives, and I had to accept that it wasn't going to ever work."

"At least she had the decency to tell you to your face."

"Yes, but that didn't erase the sting. She reminded me, though, of what I'd told myself all along. That I didn't have time for a relationship. And in the end, I let her walk away. Maybe I should have regretted it, but to be honest, I didn't."

"Which meant she wasn't the right person for you."

"No, she wasn't. You know, you're different from her."

"How?"

"You have courage. A concern for others."

"All I see is that I've been terrified this entire week. With everything that's happened, I haven't been able to shake the feeling that someone is around the corner trying to kill me."

"But you never let it stop you from doing what you have to do. And in the end, isn't that what really matters? We're all afraid of something. But how we choose to deal with that fear is what makes the difference."

Something crashed behind them. Kate jumped in her seat. "See what I mean?"

"It's just a bunch of rowdy kids who've been drinking too much."

She looked behind them at the group of college-aged students who were messing around taking photos of each other. "I know it's just . . . I can't stop looking over my shoulder."

She shivered, despite her sweater and the warm evening breeze. She'd almost managed to shake her fears tonight. Almost. But they'd found her today. And while she'd managed to get away, the next time she might not be so lucky. And just because they'd caught Davin Bernard, didn't mean things were over. If her theory was right, there was someone else involved besides Sophie's kidnappers. Someone else who was just as desperate to get their hands on five million dollars' worth of diamonds.

"I need to go to the restroom," she said, standing up.

"You want me to come with you?" he asked, starting to follow her.

"No . . . I'll just be a minute."

And she'd be fine. She was tired of jumping at every shadow.

"The Eiffel Tower is just up ahead, which means we'll be getting off soon."

Kate glanced at the tower in the distance, lit up now by hundreds of twinkling gold lights. The reminder punched through her gut. She'd be there tomorrow. Making the exchange for Sophie's life.

She passed the group of young people, drinking and photo-bombing each other's pictures. Someone jostled against her. She hurried past them, trying to shake off the feeling someone was watching her. Music played in the background, the commentator rambled on in four different languages no one could hear. They were drinking too much and dancing . . .

She maneuvered her way toward the restroom, then froze. He stood in the aisle blocking her way. She'd recognize him anywhere. Short and stocky with red curly hair. One of the men who tried to grab her near the Anne-Loure shop.

"Where are the diamonds?" he said, grasping her wrist. "I know you have them."

"Marcus!"

The man pulled her toward him. Music pulsed as he leaned close to her. "Do you actually think he can hear you in all this commotion?"

Kate's jaw tensed. "What do you want?"

"The diamonds."

"I don't understand. You set the details for the exchange."

He pulled back slightly, his hand still gripping her wrist. "What exchange?"

"I told you I would keep my side of the deal."

"There is no deal. I want the diamonds."

The music pulsed louder. Lights of the city blurred in the distance.

"I'll be at the tower," she said. "Just promise me Sophie will be safe."

Or had her theory been right, and they knew nothing about Sophie?

Kate felt someone else shove against her. She breathed in the pungent smell of alcohol as she lost her balance. The man lost hold of her wrist and grabbed for her as she screamed, but it was too late. She fell backward over the side of the boat.

For a moment Kate felt nothing, then the sharp impact of the water engulfed her as she plunged below the surface.

FIFTEEN

Marcus jumped up from his seat at the sound of someone screaming, and ran toward the commotion. His heart pounded as he tried to convince himself this had nothing to do with Kate.

A crowd had gathered at the rail. Someone yelled for the boat to stop. He scanned the deck for Kate. She was probably in the restroom, and he was panicking for nothing. But convincing himself she was fine wasn't working. He pushed his way through the passengers. He never should have let her out of his sight.

"What's going on?" he shouted in French, trying to be heard above the music.

"Some woman," a tall, blond man answered. "She was arguing with a man, then . . . I don't know what happened. She fell into the water."

Fell into the water . . . No, God, please.

"What did she look like?"

"Late twenties . . . ponytail . . ."

Kate.

Marcus searched the murky water. A spotlight from the boat caught her struggling a few meters from the boat. Without hesitating, he dived into the river after her.

The cold impact of the water sucked his breath

away. He swam to the surface, filled his lungs with air, then tried to find his bearings. People were shouting at him from the boat. He drew in another deep breath and followed the beam of the spotlight. But all he could see was water, and beyond the spotlight, darkness.

Time was running out. Where was she?

"Kate?"

The spotlight shifted. He turned toward it again, squinting. Nothing. He'd lost her.

If she'd gone under, finding her in the dark would be almost impossible.

No, God, please . . . help me find her.

He couldn't lose her. Not again. Not this way.

She surfaced a half-dozen feet from him, spewing water then sucking in air. In three broad strokes, he was beside her. He pulled her against him, ensuring her head was above the water.

"Kate?"

She was shaking, her teeth chattering.

"Kate, can you hear me?"

She nodded.

A bruise had already started forming on her forehead. She must have hit her head when she fell. He glanced back at the boat. A life preserver dropped into the water beside them. He grabbed onto it, then started swimming toward the boat.

Someone helped hoist them up onto the deck. The music had stopped, and the rowdy crowd had fallen eerily quiet. They laid Kate on the deck on a pile of cushions. Someone dropped a blanket over her.

Marcus knelt down beside her, water dripping from his clothes, and pushed back a strand of wet hair from her forehead. He needed to get her warm. Needed to get her out of here. "Kate . . . talk to me. What happened?"

She shook her head, her chest heaving, eyes wide as if trying to orient herself.

"Give yourself a minute. You're going to be okay." He pulled the blanket tighter around her shoulders and rubbed her arms with his hands, then signaled one of the crew to get them something hot to drink.

A moment later someone handed him two mugs of coffee.

"Thank you." Marcus helped her take a sip. "Tell me what happened, Kate."

"He . . . he grabbed me and started asking me questions about the diamonds," Kate said finally. "He said he knew I had them. There were so many people around us. They were loud . . . drinking. The next thing I knew someone pushed me against the railing of the boat and then I was falling."

"Who was he?"

"He . . ."

"Kate?" He needed to find whoever had pushed her over. He glanced up, surprised that the boat was already at the shore . . . In a few more minutes it would be too late. "I need you to focus. Did you recognize him?"

"Yes . . . He was the driver of the car who tried to grab me," she said.

"Did he push you?"

"There were so many people . . . I don't know . . . I think it was an accident."

Marcus turned to the blond man he'd spoken to earlier. "The man she was talking to. Did you see where he went?"

"Sorry, but there must be two hundred people on this boat."

"Can I get you something else?" The woman who'd been doing the live commentary on the boat knelt down beside them.

"I'm a federal agent working with French intelligence. I need you to ensure no one gets off this boat until I say so—"

"I'm sorry, sir, but we've just docked and the passengers are already debarking. But we did call for an ambulance. It should be here any minute."

Marcus glanced at the dock, his fists clenched beside him, and tried to restrain his growing anger. If they'd already docked, whoever was responsible for this was long gone.

Kate struggled to sit up. "I don't need to go to the hospital, Marcus. Please."

"It's just a precaution," Marcus assured her, focusing his attention back on her. "You're going to be fine."

• • •

He told her she'd be fine. And maybe she was. Physically. Emotionally she was falling apart. Someone had given her dry clothes to change into, but she was still shivering from fear as much as the cold. They'd asked her questions, tested her reflexes and determined that she didn't have a concussion. All she wanted now was to go back to the safe house, take a shower and sleep for the next twenty-four hours.

Except she couldn't.

Kate looked up as Marcus entered the small exam room, his clothes still damp.

"You ready to go?" he asked.

"Yes." She grabbed her purse from the side of the exam table. Someone had managed to pick it up for her.

"Kate, wait. Before we go . . ." He templed his hands in front of him. "I've been thinking about something."

Her gaze narrowed. "What's wrong?"

Marcus looked at her and paused.

"Did they find him?"

"No . . . It's not that . . . I want you to return to the US. I can get you on the next flight out of Charles de Gaulle. It wouldn't give you a lot of time to sleep tonight, but you could sleep on the plane—"

"Forget it." Kate started for the door, wishing the pain medicine they'd given her for her head would kick in. "I don't want to talk about this again. You know I can't return. Not now . . . not until I find Sophie."

He stepped in front of her, blocking the door. "After tonight, hasn't it been made completely clear that it's not safe for you here?"

"Sophie isn't exactly in a safe place right now, either, Marcus. I promised my sister I'd find her, and I'm not leaving her behind."

"I understand how you feel—"

"Do you?"

He took her hands, but she pulled away from him. It didn't matter what he thought. She was staying, and she was going to make the exchange.

"Kate, this is bigger than your sister and your niece. Chad was involved with diamond smugglers who are financing military-grade weapons for rebels. They don't play by the rules, Kate. They don't care if someone like you gets hurt. But I do."

She looked up at him and shook her head. "You need me here, Marcus, and you know it."

"I need you safe. I don't want anything to happen to you, Kate. What if the next time you run into them you're not so lucky?" His gaze softened. "I don't want you a part of this—"

"It's too late for that, Marcus. I'm already a part of it."

His jaw tensed as he focused on something on the wall behind her.

"Marcus?" She wanted—needed—him to understand. "I can't just walk away from this."

"I know." He bent down and kissed her gently on the forehead. "I know."

She reached up and ran her hand down his arm, wishing they were somewhere else. Anywhere else but here. Because despite her words—and his protection—she still had to fight the urge not to run. Men who didn't blink at snatching a young girl from her mother *didn't* care about who got hurt. They'd diminished the value of human life to a handful of shiny rocks.

"What will you do now?" she asked, thankful he wasn't still arguing with her.

"I'll have Jocelyn take you back to the safe house. I'm going back down to the station to talk with Davin Bernard. See if I can find a way to get some information out of him. I'm still convinced he has to know something about Sophie. If we can find out who's involved it will up the odds that things go our way tomorrow."

"Do you think she's okay?" It was a question she shouldn't be asking, but she couldn't help it. She needed reassurance. Something positive to hold on to.

"I don't know the answer to that, Kate, but I do know that they need her until they get the diamonds."

Kate repositioned her purse strap on her shoulder, trying to control the constant worry in her gut. That would have to be enough for the moment. “Sophie turns five next week. Rachel was planning to throw her a party. She let Sophie pick out the cake, and the plates and cups. Sent out invitations to her friends. If they hurt her, Marcus . . .”

He pressed his finger gently against her lips. “Don’t go there. You saw the photo. They need to keep her safe.”

“But she has to be so scared. The time she’s not with Rachel, she’s with me or my mom. She’s never been away from home like this.”

“I know this is hard, Kate, but we’re going to get her back. And as for you, I want you to get to the safe house and get some sleep. Tomorrow is going to be a long day.”

Marcus walked into the police station, where he’d arranged to talk with Davin Bernard. On his way, he’d called Jocelyn to ensure Kate was settled into the safe house. At least Kate hadn’t argued this time about staying behind. Knowing she was safe for the moment would allow him to concentrate on putting an end to all of this.

“Heard you took a little swim.”

Marcus glanced down at his rumpled clothes, frowning at Pierre’s comment in the dingy hallway of the police station. “Yeah . . . not exactly how I intended to spend my evening.”

“I can imagine. Sailing down the Seine with a

beautiful woman in the most beautiful city in the world. That's not how I'd want it to end, either." Pierre chuckled, but his grin quickly faded. "How is she?"

"Holding on." Marcus ignored the other man's implications. He might be on track, but he wasn't interested in giving Pierre fuel for the fire. "Jocelyn drove her back to the apartment to get cleaned up and hopefully get some sleep. This hasn't exactly been a great day for her."

Or a great week for either of them, for that matter. As far as he was concerned, things had continually gone from bad to worse. He was hoping that the man sitting inside the interrogation room was about to change all of that.

"She seems to be quite a woman," Pierre said as they started down the hall to interrogation room three.

"Kate?"

"As if you didn't know. I can see it in your eyes."

"It's my duty to protect her."

"Your duty or your desire?"

Marcus frowned. "It's the same thing, isn't it?"

"Like I said, I can see it in your eyes."

"I've known her a total of what . . . four days? And most of that time has been spent running."

He wasn't claiming he didn't have feelings for her. But neither was he going to ignore the possibility that everything could change when they returned home. When emotions died down and things went back to normal. When she didn't need him anymore as her protector.

"Days, weeks, months . . ." Pierre said. "Sometimes it doesn't matter. Sometimes you just know. I felt the same way about my wife when we first met. Took me a while to admit she was the one for me, but I knew it." Pierre tapped him on the back as they stopped in front of the interrogation room door. "Besides, you are in Paris."

Paris.

Marcus pulled the door open, wondering if he'd ever see Paris the same way again if he didn't have Kate at his side.

Inside the small, drab room, Marcus forced his mind to concentrate as he slid into one of the two empty seats across from their suspect. Davin Bernard rubbed his goatee, clearly annoyed to have been brought in for questioning at this time of the night.

"It's good to see you again, Davin," Marcus began in French. "You remember me?"

"I remember I had nothing to say the last time I saw you."

"Well, things have changed. We thought we'd give you another chance to tell us why you took a woman at gunpoint this morning."

"What exactly has changed?"

Marcus slapped down the man's file onto the

table in front of him. "We ran into your partner tonight. Thankfully, he's not quite as stubborn as you are. He's considering making a deal in exchange for telling us what we want to know about the diamonds and giving us names." He kept his gaze steady. There was no reason why Monsieur Bernard needed to know they didn't yet have his partner in custody. "You, on the other hand, will be charged with the kidnapping of four-year-old Sophie Laurent, the attempted murder of Rachel Laurent, along with a long list of other crimes we plan to pin on you, including what happened this morning with Kate Elliot."

"No way." The man smacked his hands against the table. "You're lying."

"Really?" Pierre asked. "I don't think so."

Davin rubbed his hands across the sides of his head. "I admit to grabbing the woman from the apartment this morning—and even trying to grab her off the street yesterday, but that is all. I didn't kidnap no kid or try to murder the man's wife."

"Then tell me what you know, or you're going to take the fall for all of it," Pierre said.

Davin dropped his hands and started drumming his fingers against the table. His gaze dropped. "I knew Chad. Worked for him a few times."

"Doing what?" Marcus asked.

"I'm a . . . a businessman? I have resources people need."

"Like?"

Davin hesitated again.

Marcus leaned forward. "This is a limited deal we're offering you, so I'd make up your mind quickly as to whether or not you're going to save your skin, or if your friend is going to get the deal and let you rot the rest of your life in prison."

Davin shoved back his chair. "Fine. Chad hired me to steal six music boxes from his wife's house in Texas."

"Why?"

"He didn't tell me. I didn't ask."

"But you were curious. It was a strange request."

"Chad worked with diamonds. I figured they must be worth something. He promised to pay me a hundred grand if I found them."

"And so when you got to the house, you decided a hundred grand wasn't enough? That if you took Chad's daughter you could use her as leverage and make him pay a whole lot more—"

"No. I told you, I didn't take the kid. The house was empty when I got there. I made sure of it. I never saw Rachel or her daughter. But the music boxes weren't there. Whoever shot his wife and took his kid had to have shown up after I was there."

Which meant if he was telling the truth, someone else was involved.

"And when you told Chad you couldn't find the diamonds?" Marcus asked.

"He started freaking out, all panicked."

"Do you know why?"

"I figured he needed them because he owed someone something."

Five million dollars' worth of diamonds.

"What happened next?" Pierre asked.

"Chad told me without the music boxes he couldn't pay me. All he could do was cover my expenses, so Wednesday morning, once I was back in the country, I went to his work to confront him. That's when I saw her. I thought it was his wife. Thought if I used her as leverage, Chad would change his mind."

"So you don't kidnap children, but you're not against kidnapping in general?"

Davin's frown deepened. "I knew he was sitting on something huge. Something I wanted a part of. I started poking around a bit. I knew Chad bought rough diamonds from mining fields in Zimbabwe and other places in Africa. And eventually, Chad confirmed it."

"How did you get him to confess?"

"Told him I was the one who had Sophie. The guy was terrified. He told me he had been working as an illegal wholesaler on the side."

"And you . . . as a businessman . . . decided you needed a cut."

"Who wouldn't? He works at a loss, but still

makes plenty of money. I figured the music boxes were filled with diamonds he'd been skimming off the top."

"Apparently, you're not the only one who came to that conclusion. Do you know who really kidnapped Chad's daughter, Sophie Laurent?"

Davin shrugged. "Chad was in deep, and I'm sure he had more than one buyer. He picked up the rough diamonds in Africa and smuggled them into France then sold the undocumented diamonds to foreign buyers. South Africans. Russians. Lebanese. He was cheating his bosses, and I'm sure he had a number of enemies."

A moment later, Pierre signaled for Marcus to join him in the hallway. "What do you think?"

Marcus rubbed the back of his head. "I think he's telling the truth, which means Kate was right. We're looking at more than one person who's after those diamonds."

Which complicated everything. Because tomorrow was the exchange, and they still didn't know who had Sophie.

SIXTEEN

At ten-thirty, Marcus walked beside Kate along Pont d'Iéna, the bridge that linked the Eiffel Tower, located on the Left Bank, to the district of Tracadéro on the Right Bank, with the diamonds in hand. Blood diamonds. Conflict diamonds. Smuggled then sold as legitimate gems. It wasn't supposed to happen. But it did. They'd funded organized crime, corrupt regimes and international terrorist organizations. Funded war, genocide and slavery.

He glanced at Kate. He could tell from the stiffness of her shoulders and the quiver in her voice when she spoke that her nerves were on edge.

"Are you sure you want to go through with this?" he asked.

"Stop asking me that question."

"I can bring in another agent. Same build and body type. We can make it work."

Kate shook her head. He might be stubborn, but clearly so was she. "You know I have to do this."

"They're criminals. They don't play by the rules, Kate."

She sighed. "I know."

"Fine. We'll do everything in our power to

ensure you get her back. I can promise you that."

"Then arrest them. This . . ." she said. "This needs to stop."

"Maybe you've been called for such a time as this," he said, quoting from the book of Esther.

"Maybe."

Evil would always be there, but maybe they could win this one.

He wrapped his hand around hers. "I know how hard this has been for you. I'm always amazed at how much more strength people have than they realize. Sometimes you have to dig, Kate, but you have that kind of strength."

"I just hope it lasts. I feel as if I'm running on adrenaline and fumes. Eventually it's going to run out."

"All you need is enough for right now."

They'd gone over what was going to happen a dozen times before Pierre had driven them to an intersection near the Eiffel Tower, where Kate would make the exchange.

"Did you know that Napoleon I ordered the construction of this bridge over two hundred years ago?" he asked, above the noisy crowd on the bridge.

Hawkers insisted they buy miniature versions of the tower and other souvenirs. Musicians played for change to the tourists.

"No. I didn't know that." Her voice was flat.

"It was named after the general who won the

Battle of Jena," he continued. "Eight years after its construction, though, General Blücher decided to destroy the bridge before the Battle of Paris."

"Obviously he didn't."

Marcus chuckled despite the heaviness hanging between them. "He was eventually persuaded by the Allied forces not to destroy it."

She stopped at an empty spot along the edge overlooking the Seine and shook her head. "It would have been a shame to have destroyed it, though I suppose if it didn't live in the shadow of the Eiffel Tower, it probably would be just another bridge."

"The bridge itself isn't spectacular, but you're right. You can get some incredible photos of the Eiffel Tower from here."

She glanced at her watch, something she'd been doing every minute for the past hour.

"Kate?"

"I'm fine."

She started walking again, but he grasped her arm gently and pulled her toward him. "Watching the time isn't going to speed things up, Kate. We have plenty of time for you to get to the tower and to the second level."

She stopped and looked over the edge of the bridge at the Seine without responding. The Eiffel Tower loomed in the background, the iconic symbol of Paris originally built for the 1889 World's Fair that today attracted more visitors than any other paid tourist attraction in the world.

But she already knew all of that. They weren't here to visit one of France's most enduring landmarks. They were here in hopes of saving Sophie's life. But putting Kate in the middle of the exchange wasn't something he was convinced they should do.

He'd gone over their demands a dozen times. Twelve o'clock. Second level of the Eiffel Tower. Don't be late. Come alone.

Which meant no cops, no FBI agents, no French security. And no matter how many times they'd gone over every possible scenario, he still didn't like it. But sometimes, like today, there was nothing else he could do.

"Hey . . ." He reached up and ran his thumb down her cheek. "We're going to get Sophie back."

Kate nodded while tears pooled in her eyes, clearly afraid if she said anything more she'd break down crying. Or maybe take him up on his offer to let someone else take her place. But she'd insisted they knew who she was. She couldn't risk going against their demands with Sophie's life on the line.

"You know the plan?" He didn't need to ask her again, but he did anyway.

She nodded. "I make the exchange and get down to the ground level as quickly as I can with Sophie."

"And if anything goes wrong? If Sophie isn't there, or they change plans—"

"I tug on my scarf."

"And I'll be right there. I promise."

She nodded, still avoiding his gaze.

He glanced down at her outfit, which Jocelyn had helped put together. Layered white and yellow tank top, blue jeans and bright blue scarf topped off with a pair of sunglasses and flats. With her tie-dyed bag and camera in hand, she looked just like any other tourist ready to take on the City of Lights. Not a young woman whose entire world had just been ripped out from under her.

"They have to know their plan is risky, trying to make an exchange in such a public, crowded place," she said.

"That's what they are counting on. The tower *is* going to be crowded. They are hoping to use that advantage to slip away with the diamonds. There is liable to be a handoff, so we have to be ready, and make sure we don't lose them."

She nodded.

"You have a microphone, so we can hear you, and we'll be close by, I promise. We're hoping the crowd will work to our advantage."

She nodded again.

"As soon as they walk away, you describe them to me."

"I will."

"And as soon as you have Sophie, you head for the elevator toward the ground floor. Walk back this way toward the bridge. I'll be there to pick you both up."

She looked up at him and slid her sunglasses back on. "And you'll arrest the men who took her?"

"That's the plan. There's also the woman who passed herself off as Rachel. We'll be looking for her, as well."

Kate shivered despite the warm weather. "I remember the night before Sophie was born. There were complications that came up, and while the doctor was vague about his concerns, it was clear he was worried. She was born, twenty-four hours later, absolutely perfect. No problems. Just a sweet, beautiful baby girl. I don't think I've ever seen Rachel so happy. Which is funny in a way. She'd been terrified that she wouldn't make a good mother. All of those fears seemed to vanish when she held Sophie for the first time."

They started walking again, ignoring the hawkers still trying to sell them souvenirs. "When all of this is over, I'd like the chance to show you the city. Maybe a bike tour . . . espressos in one of the cafés . . . and an afternoon in the Louvre."

There was a hint of a smile in her eyes for the first time all morning. "I'd like that."

He knew he was trying to calm her nerves. Trying to get her to think about something else, anything except the fact that she was about to meet her niece's kidnapper and make an exchange with a possible terrorist.

He stopped again and leaned toward her, breathing in the faint scent of her perfume, and brushed his lips across hers. "We're going to find her."

She nodded and gave him a slight smile, "Good, because I'm holding you to that promise."

Kate waited in the long line, jostled by the eager crowds. She'd arrived early as she'd wanted to, anticipating the long lines of people going up to the tower and giving herself an hour and a half to get through the lines and up the elevator. She'd considered walking up the seven hundred steps to the second level, but the way her legs were shaking she knew she'd never make it. She scanned the crowd as the line moved forward, but there was no sign of Sophie. More than likely they were already up in the tower anticipating her arrival. Hopefully, they'd buy her niece lunch to pass the time, but more than likely the restaurant didn't serve mac and cheese.

She knew Sophie would be scared without her mother. The only familiar thing she had was Lily, her one-eyed bunny. But this would all be over soon. All she had to do was buy her ticket . . . take the elevator to the top . . . find Sophie . . . and give them the diamonds.

Marcus would handle the rest.

God, I feel as if You brought Marcus into my life at such a time as this to be that one, tangible source of strength You knew I would need. Thank You for him. For his concern and compassion. And help him and the others to find these guys who have tried so hard to destroy our family.

She neared the ticket counter and let her thoughts shift to Marcus. He had become her anchor in the storm. The unexpected part of the equation that had managed to help set her world right again. Almost. But she wasn't going to fool herself into thinking that as soon as she had Sophie they'd somehow ride off into the sunset together.

Instead, she'd leave France and return to her studies. Life would take on its normal rhythm again with mundane things like grocery shopping and picking up her dry cleaning. Marcus O'Brian wasn't a part of that life.

But could he be?

She still wasn't sure. She shook her head as she walked up to the ticket counter and gave the woman exact change for her ticket, keeping one hand on the diamonds nestled safely in her bag. They might have a lot in common—including their faith—but the attraction she felt toward him wasn't enough to build a relationship on.

She shoved her wondering thoughts of Marcus from her mind, told the attendant *merci*, then headed toward the elevator. She glanced at her watch. She still had forty-five minutes until she was supposed to meet them.

All she could do now was pray that nothing went wrong.

Marcus started up the stairs, two at a time toward the second level of the Eiffel Tower. His heart was already pounding by the time he reached the second set of stairs, but more from anxiety than the exertion.

He passed a group of schoolchildren coming down the stairs with their backpacks while their teachers lagged behind. Jocelyn was following Kate up the elevator, but he wanted to be on the second level before she got there. Whoever was making the pickup would more than likely be there already. They needed photographs of the crowd in case they missed grabbing them.

Doubts over their strategy had begun this morning and continued as they'd plotted out the remaining details. Guilt nagged. What if they'd overlooked something? Some detail that they hadn't considered?

He hated situations like this. When so much was out of his hands.

I need a way to bring both Kate and Sophie to safety, God.

Because once again he was second-guessing his decisions.

Which wasn't like him.

He'd participated in dozens of arrests. Handoffs and exchanges. But Kate had managed to dig under his skin and go straight for his heart. A place he'd managed to keep guarded until now. He wanted things to go right, not just because he wanted justice done in this situation, but because he truly cared about her.

That determination in her eyes had him falling for her. And when all of this was over, he simply wasn't ready to have her fly back to the United States without telling her how he felt. Her kiss had magnified the chemistry between them, and managed to push him over that invisible edge of no return.

Seventeen minutes later, he passed the last information board and stepped onto the second level of the tower, thankful he wasn't afraid of heights. Camera in hand, he started taking photos like all the other tourists. Except he wasn't looking at the panoramic view of the city below. He was looking for Sophie.

They'd rehearsed the exchange, following the script the kidnappers had sent them.

"Excuse me, do you have any change for the binoculars? My niece wants to look through them, and I don't have any change."

Kate would set her bag down with the

diamonds then hand the woman change for the vintage coin-operated binoculars . . .

He glanced across the floor to where Pierre was videotaping, then glanced at his watch. Twenty-five more minutes, and all of this would be over.

Kate's stomach lurched as the glass elevator ascended inside the metal structure. She hung on to one of the poles, listening to the different languages being spoken around her, but staring past the crowd that was packed into the confined space. People videotaped the ascent, as the pedestrians below got smaller by the second.

But she felt none of their enthusiasm. Instead, nausea swept over her. Her fingers tightened around the pole, certain everyone knew why she was here. A man announced everyone must get off and change elevators. She stepped off automatically, barely seeing the restaurant and gift shop.

Sophie was here somewhere. Among the tourists with their bags and backpacks, cameras and camcorders. Pressed together like sardines in order to capture a bird's-eye view of the city.

Kate glanced at her watch as she stepped out onto the second level. She was five minutes early. Which meant they were here, somewhere. She tried not to panic. Tried not to imagine what would happen if they didn't show up.

Her hands began to sweat. The bag she was

carrying felt heavier. Maybe Marcus had been right. She wasn't exactly an agent, or a trained officer with knowledge of what to do in a situation like this.

She stepped up beside one of the binoculars that overlooked the Arc de Triomphe and the Champs Elysées that stretched from it, but she wasn't here for the view.

She looked out over the crowd. Snapped a photo of the view. Marcus was here, along with half a dozen plainclothes officers. She just wanted it to be over.

Please, Lord. Let me find Sophie.

She pulled her bag against her side and shot up a prayer. Something she'd been doing all morning. Marcus had assured her that he and his team would be there, just as they had when she'd met Chad.

But that meeting had ended in tragedy. She couldn't let anything happen today. Five million dollars' worth of diamonds and a little girl's life were at stake. This had to work.

"Sophie!"

"Auntie Kate—"

Kate watched the woman holding her hand cut her off and shake her head. Kate glanced around her at the crowd. No one had a clue what was going on.

Surely they wouldn't do anything to Sophie here. Not in front of hundreds of witnesses.

Please, God. Get us through the next few minutes until I can get Sophie out of here safely.

The woman holding Sophie's hand approached her with a frown on her face. "Do you have change for the binoculars? My niece hasn't seen the view before, and I forgot to bring any change."

Kate nodded, her hands shaking. She set her bag down beside her then started digging for the coin she'd left in her pocket. "I've got some . . . It's here somewhere."

She wanted to scream at the guard to help.

"I wouldn't try anything if I were you. I'm not here alone. And you wouldn't want anything to happen to your niece."

Kate nodded, then handed her the coin before taking Sophie's hand. "I think you have what you need now."

He had watched the woman approach her. Kate nodded. Marcus snapped a photo. Two could play this game, as well. Sophie's smile had broadened as she'd caught sight of her aunt. The woman holding her hand had pulled her toward her, causing Sophie's smile to vanish. But not for long. The girl looked as if she hadn't been harmed, but there was no way to tell at this point.

The woman glanced at the binoculars, and said something to Kate.

Kate nodded, set down her bag, then dug for a coin in her pocket.

The woman picked up the bag, quickly inspected the contents of the bag, then let go of Sophie's hand.

"Describe her to me, Kate," Marcus said as the woman walked away.

"Twenty-five . . . maybe a bit older. Reddish-brown hair that looks as if it's been colored. A narrow scar above her right eyebrow. Dark blue capri pants. White T-shirt."

"Good girl. What's she doing?"

"Walking toward the stairs."

"Keep your eye on her, team. We don't want to lose her, or those diamonds." Marcus had his attention on Kate and Sophie. "It's the easy part now, Kate. Head for the elevator. I'll meet you down below."

Marcus saw her walk toward the elevators. A large group of Japanese tourists congregated in front of him, blocking his view.

"Kate? Kate? Can you hear me?"

"Yes. We're headed to the elevators."

Marcus was right behind her. "Jocelyn . . . have you still got our kidnapper in your sights?"

"Got her. So far everything seems to be going along as planned."

"Pierre?"

"I'm right behind her."

Someone bumped into him. Kate had vanished from his sight.

"Kate? Where are you?"

They'd been less than twenty feet from him three seconds ago. He scanned the growing crowd, trying not to panic. Everyone was headed for the stairs. The loudspeaker blasted out instructions for everyone to calmly take the stairs.

He spoke into his microphone. "What's going on, Pierre?"

"They're evacuating the tower."

"I can see that. Why?"

"I don't know."

Security was signaling people toward the stairs, ordering everyone to calmly leave the tower.

"Do you see her, Jocelyn?"

"I lost her, and she's not responding."

"Kate?"

Why wasn't she answering? She had to be here. Somewhere. There wasn't anywhere else for her to go except down the flight of stairs with the rest of the tourists.

Kate grabbed Sophie tightly as she walked toward the elevators. "Sophie . . . I've missed you so much. Are you okay? Did they hurt you?"

"No. They fed me macaroni and cheese." Sophie clutched her one-eyed bunny and nodded. "Where's my mommy?"

Kate's heart tripped. "You and I are going to take a long plane trip and see her, okay?"

"I don't like airplanes."

"But this time, you'll get to see Mommy, okay?"

But not until they got out of here. The quickest way down was probably the stairs, but with Sophie, the elevators would be the easiest. Marcus would meet them below. Everything had gone as planned. She had Sophie and they'd both be on the next flight out of here.

The announcement blasted over the loudspeaker system. "Ladies and gentlemen, the tower is closed. We need you to take the stairs down to the ground."

The crowd grew around her. Bumped into her. Glancing down below, she could see where police had set up a barricade. She tugged on the arm of one of the security guards who was passing by her. "I'm sorry . . . what's going on?"

The guard turned to her and frowned. "Everyone must evacuate the tower immediately. There's been a bomb threat."

SEVENTEEN

A bomb threat?

Kate's mouth went dry. She'd gone through all the possible scenarios over and over with Marcus and Jocelyn. But not a bomb. Why had they not thought of the possibility of a bomb?

She knew the authorities took threats seriously, but surely this was just a coincidence. She glanced around them, looking for the team of security Marcus had brought with him. They had to be here, but no one looked familiar.

She squeezed Sophie's hand. She'd simply stick to the plan and meet Marcus at the bottom of the tower. The line to the elevator had dissolved as everyone crowded toward the staircase. Kate felt a wave of nausea as she looked over the edge. They were a hundred and fifteen feet above the ground. A bomb could destroy the entire tower in a matter of seconds.

There isn't a real bomb. It's just a ploy by the kidnappers to add to the confusion . . .

"Marcus . . . Marcus . . ." She pressed her hand against the wire they'd placed under her scarf. It was gone. No . . . no . . . It must have fallen off in all of the chaos.

Sophie tugged on Kate's arm. "I don't want to take the stairs."

"Just think of it as another game, Sophie." Kate forced a smile. Without any way to communicate, she was on her own. "It will be fun, don't you think?"

"Where's my mommy, Auntie Kate? I want to go home."

Tears spilled down Sophie's cheeks.

"It's going to be okay, sweetie. Those bad people who took you are going to go to jail, but you're safe."

Sophie's lip quivered.

"But to go see your mom, we need to walk down the stairs."

"Okay," she said finally.

"Did you come up on this tower when you were in Paris with your mother?" Kate asked as they started down the stairs.

Sophie nodded. "We ate lunch at the restaurant, where Mommy took lots of pictures with me and *Grand-père*."

Kate helped maneuver Sophie through the heavy crowds. "Would you like to see your *grand-père* again?"

"He always buys me ice cream, and promised to take me on the carousel."

"Well, I think that would be fun." People were pushing against them again. Kate tightened her grip on Sophie's hand, making sure she still had her bunny. "Can you guess how many steps to the bottom?"

Sophie shook her head.

"How high can you count?" Kate asked instead.

"One hundred."

"Then let's start there. Just hold my hand tightly, and count."

They continued down the stairs near the back of the crowd. If the woman who had taken Sophie was in the crowd, she couldn't see her.

An explosive detection team with dogs was coming up on the elevator.

If there really were a bomb . . .

Kate tried to swallow the worry. Worry they'd grab Sophie again. Worry this wasn't just a threat.

Please, God . . . You brought us this far safely. I need You to keep us safe.

Kate looked down at her niece, who'd quit counting. "Stay close to me, okay, Sophie? And hold tight to your bunny."

Seven million visitors a year.

Up to 30,000 a day in the summer.

Was this part of the kidnappers' plan, or just a coincidence?

Kate considered the question as they continued down the stairs.

Bomb threats weren't uncommon, but there was no doubt in her mind that this had been their plan all along. They'd likely have passed off the diamonds into a different package and in the chaos, expect to make a clean getaway.

You can't let that happen, God.

Kate looked for Marcus as they exited the tower at the bottom of the stairs a few minutes later and melted into the crowd. Two policemen on bikes crossed in front of them. A large roll of tape, like for a crime scene, but with red writing, had been stretched out across the entrance.

Jocelyn appeared in front of her among the hundreds of tourists. "I've been looking everywhere for you. We need to get you out of here. I've got a car waiting out on the street."

"Where's Marcus? This wasn't the plan."

He was supposed to be here. She needed him here.

"Neither was a bomb threat. Please. I know you're scared, but I want to get you out of here and keep you safe. And you must be Sophie," Jocelyn said as they wove through the crowds.

Sophie nodded and gripped Kate's hand even tighter.

"Did you get them?" Kate asked.

"We will. We have photos circulating and arrest warrants out for the woman who had Sophie."

Kate's stomach soured. The kidnappers' plan had worked. They'd gotten away.

"I'm working to get you a flight out of the country," Jocelyn said.

"And Marcus?"

"He'll meet us at the safe house," she said as they hurried across the crowded plaza.

Sophie stumbled. "I can't walk so fast."

Kate picked her up, and hurried behind Jocelyn. Sophie nuzzled against her shoulder, her bunny tucked tightly beneath her chin.

"How is she?" Jocelyn asked as they hurried through the mass of tourists where police were trying to make order of the chaos.

"She seems okay," Kate said, "She misses her mom."

"I don't blame her. It's hard to imagine what she went through."

A man stopped in front of them, blocking their way. Kate started to move around him, then froze. It was him. The crowd . . . the tower . . . everything began to spin around her. The redheaded man who had grabbed her along the Champs Elysées. The man who'd grabbed her on the Bateaux-Mouche.

He grabbed Kate's arm before she could react, then pulled out a gun. "Don't move, or I'll shoot the little girl."

She tried to turn her body to shield Sophie. His grip tightened. Someone behind them screamed, "Gun." The crowd around them scattered.

"I'm here to collect the diamonds."

Marcus searched the crowd for the woman fitting the description Kate had given him of the kidnapper. Pierre had seen the woman hand off the diamonds to a man wearing a white dress shirt and gray suit, who had slipped the jewels into a leather pouch. Whether the bomb threat was real or simply staged didn't matter at this point. Kate was out of harm's way and headed to the safe house with Sophie and Jocelyn. His role was to find the kidnappers and put an end to all of this.

"You're going to miss having me on your team after we close this case, Pierre," Marcus said over his radio, searching through the crowd for the kidnappers. They had to find them before they disappeared for good.

"Or maybe it's Kate Elliot whom you're going to miss," Pierre came back.

"I'm sure once she gets back home to her family she'll forget all about me."

"I wouldn't be so sure about that."

At least she was safe for now.

"I've still got Kate, Marcus," Jocelyn broke in, "but we've got company. South side, near the street—"

Their communication went dead.

"Jocelyn?"

Marcus pushed his way through the crowds that were slowly beginning to disperse after the evacuation.

"Pierre, did you hear that? We've got a problem."

"I'm on my way."

They were walking toward the street when Marcus found them. The description of the gunman matched the redheaded man who'd tried to grab Kate along the Champs Elysées. And the same man who'd approached her on the boat. Kate carried Sophie in front of the man. Jocelyn walked beside them.

This was not going to turn out well—at least it wasn't for the gunman. Did the guy really think the chance he was taking was worth five million dollars?

Marcus pushed his way through the crowd, came around in front of them, then caught Jocelyn's eye and nodded. A moment later, she flung herself around, taking the man by surprise, and forcing the man's arm with the gun into the air. Marcus grabbed the gun while Pierre snatched Sophie and dropped to the ground, pulling her out of the line of fire.

It was over before the gunman had a chance to realize what had happened.

"Where are the diamonds?" he shouted. "Chad and Davin promised me a cut of the diamonds."

Pierre handcuffed the man's hands behind him. "Too bad, because she doesn't have them. She never did have them, though I'll give you credit for your persistence."

Marcus turned to Kate. "Let's get you out of here."

Kate helped Sophie down from the old-fashioned carousel with its green roof in the middle of the Jardin du Luxembourg. She breathed in a deep breath of warm, summer air. She and Chad's father had brought Sophie to the park while Marcus worked with Pierre and Jocelyn to finish up their paperwork.

Seven hours ago, French police had arrested a French couple hired by Chad's boss to kidnap Sophie as leverage to get the diamonds Chad had been skimming. Thanks to the work of Marcus's team and Chad's paper trail and list of contacts, five more had been arrested and the diamonds seized. Which meant she and Sophie were safe. A fact Kate had to keep reminding herself, over and over.

Sophie was safe.

Rachel was going to live.

Kate smiled up at Sophie, catching the young girl's wide grin. "What did you think?"

"Can I go again?"

"Again? You've already gone three times."

Emotion tugged at Kate's heart as she ran her hand across one of the weatherworn wooden animals dating back to the late nineteen hundreds, before stepping off the carousel with Sophie.

She squeezed her niece's hand. "There's someone I'd like you to meet first. He's standing over there with your grandfather."

Sophie stopped. "Who is he?"

A shadow crossed Sophie's face. It was going to take time for her to feel secure again, especially around new people.

"His name is Marcus O'Brian. He's a . . . a friend of mine."

"Is he nice?"

Kate nodded. "Very nice. Remember, he's one of the men who helped rescue you."

Kate's heart tripped as they walked up to the pair, her eyes on Marcus.

He pulled off his sunglasses and smiled. "Kate. Sophie. I'm sorry it took so long for me to get here."

"That's okay. We've been having a great time, haven't we, Sophie?"

Her niece beamed. "We played at the playground and rented a toy sailboat and pushed it around with a long pole. *Grand-père* taught me how to do that. And I rode the carousel."

Kate laughed. "Three times."

"Sounds like fun." Marcus winked at Kate then knelt down in front of Sophie. "It's nice to meet you, Sophie. I've heard a lot about you."

"Auntie Kate told me about you, too."

"She did, did she?" Marcus looked up at Kate, who felt her face blush. "And what exactly has she been telling you?"

"That you are nice, and handsome, and—"

"I believe ice cream was next on our list, wasn't it, Sophie?" Kate broke in.

"I did promise Sophie I would take her for some ice cream." M. Laurent grasped Sophie's hand. "Why don't you and Agent O'Brian enjoy the rest of the afternoon together, Kate. It's a beautiful day, and Sophie and I will be fine on our own for a while."

Kate glanced at Marcus, who looked keen on the idea, before turning back to Sophie's grandfather. "Are you sure you don't mind, M. Laurent?"

"Not at all. I'm planning to soak up every moment we have together."

Sophie beamed at her grandfather.

"Don't worry about us," the older man insisted. "We can meet up later this evening. I have a granddaughter to spoil."

Kate watched Sophie and her grandfather walk away hand in hand as if they'd been friends forever. "Aren't you busy wrapping things up here?"

"I have the afternoon and evening off, actually, and I understand your flight was delayed."

"We won't be able to leave until the morning."

"Maybe that's not such a bad thing."

Her heart fluttered. As much as she wanted to get home, her heart wasn't ready to say goodbye. "Really? And why is that?'

"I don't know. Paris has always been a magical place, but one that's always more enjoyable to spend time in with someone else. So I wondered if you were up to a bit of sightseeing. M. Laurent wants to spend some extra time with Sophie, so the timing seems perfect."

Kate folded her arms across her chest. “Did you arrange this, Agent O’Brian?”

“The flight delay? I don’t have that kind of power.” He shot her a sheepish grin. “But after everything that has happened, I’m glad I don’t have to say goodbye quite yet.”

She looked up at him, suddenly feeling shy. “I’d like that.”

Because she couldn’t have chosen a more perfect setting than the timeless garden. Its green lawns spread out around them, along with winding paths, and flower beds laid out in a geometrical pattern.

“How do you think she’s doing?” Marcus asked as they started walking.

“Amazing after all she’s been through. We spent the morning together, took a walk and played in the sunshine. I haven’t told her everything about her mother, or her father, for that matter. Just that her mother is sick, and we’re going to go see her very, very soon.”

“It won’t be easy, but she has a wonderful support system,” Marcus said.

“My mom has a great trauma counselor lined up for her once we get back to Dallas. I want to let Rachel tell her about Chad, and in the meantime, until we leave, either I or her grandfather will be with her.”

“Did you know that this garden was created in 1612?” He stopped as they came to the octagonal pond in the middle of the park. "There is an old orchard, an apiary if you want to learn about beekeeping and even a spectacular collection of orchids and roses."

Kate laughed. "You really could have been a tour guide. It's beautiful here. Peaceful."

"I've always loved history. Paris was the perfect classroom." His expression softened as he looked out across the manicured grounds. "But what about you? How are you doing?"

"Honestly," she said, "my emotions seem to swing from moment to moment. Relief. Fatigue. Mainly I'm just anxious to get home. I woke up in the night terrified until I prayed and reminded myself this was over. But today, I've noticed that I haven't stopped looking behind me to see if someone is following me."

"Those feelings will eventually go away."

She looked up at him and caught his gaze. "You got them . . . all of them."

"Yes, especially after they began turning on each other. We have enough to charge them with so that they will all spend a lot of time behind bars. Kidnapping, attempted murder, smuggling, arms dealing . . ."

"I do have one regret in all of this."

"What is that?"

"I haven't really seen Paris. Not the way I'd always imagined seeing it, anyway."

The truth was, though, that it was more than

Paris she wasn't ready to leave behind. It was Marcus. They might live in the same city back in the United States, but getting on that plane still seemed like the first and last step in saying goodbye to Paris and what had happened between them.

"You will," he said. "One day."

They started walking again. "I'm going to miss Paris, but I think all I want to do right now is go home and put all of this behind me. And since Rachel is finally awake, she will need a lot of care. I'm thinking about moving in with them for the next few weeks. Just until she is able to go back to work."

"You're a good sister, but there's another reason I'm going to miss Paris," Marcus said.

"What is that?"

"I met this girl in Paris. There's something . . . different about her."

Kate couldn't help but smile. "Really?"

"In spite of the fear, she managed to help me break a case and ensure lives were saved."

"Sounds rather heroic."

"She is."

"I meant you." She stopped and turned toward him. "So you weren't just playing the role of the romantic hero?"

She hadn't been able to stop thinking about their kiss. Marcus had stolen her heart, and she was pretty sure she didn't want it back. But just because he'd kissed her, just because he'd rescued her, didn't mean he was looking for something more.

They'd leave, and that would be it.

Or would it?

"What are you thinking?" she asked, barely above a whisper.

"I was thinking that we've both been hurt. That I've spent years making excuses as to why not to fall in love. You've made me want to take that chance again."

"Then what happens now? If we both decide to take a chance?" Her breath caught as she sought to capture the magic of the moment. Music played in the background from a nearby gazebo. The summer breeze played with her hair. The setting was perfect. The moment . . . perfect.

"We both go home," he said. "Start a relationship the way normal people do. Dinner, walks in the park, a movie or two. And we see what happens."

"No kidnappings, or smugglers, or gun-runners?" she asked.

Marcus laughed. "Just you and me and boring suburbia."

"Until you're off on another case."

"I like the idea of having someone to come back to. And for now . . . for now, though, I thought it was time you saw Paris in a different light."

Kate looked up at him, feeling enchanted.

"Because Paris should be spent with someone you enjoy being with," he continued. "Strolling along the Left Bank. Maybe into the Latin Quarter. Paris has some incredible antique bookstores, you know, and charming cafés. And you haven't really seen the Eiffel Tower at night—since the last time you tried swimming in the Seine. It's dressed with twinkling lights that turn on every hour."

Kate laughed, took a step forward and rested her hand against his chest.

Everything else—and everyone else—seemed to vanish around them.

"It might sound silly," she said, "but there was a time when I thought my chance for love was over. That I'd lost my one chance. But now . . . it's as if all of that has changed."

"Good, because I'm ready to put aside my excuses and give this—give us—a try."

She'd always dreamed of coming to Paris. Imagined it being full of wonder and romance. But something struck her as he reached down, wrapped his arms around her and kissed her in the middle of the City of Lights. It didn't really matter where they were. As long as they were together.

EPILOGUE

Sophie met Kate and Marcus at the front door of Rachel's home, still clad in her purple pajamas and carrying Lily.

"Auntie Kate!" she squealed.

"Still in your pajamas?" Kate dropped her spare key into her purse then drew her niece into a bear hug and laughed. After two weeks back in the United States, she still had to constantly remind herself that Sophie really was safe. "It's almost lunchtime, silly girl."

"Mommy said I could stay in my pajamas all day, if I want. Like a slumber party."

"Well, a slumber party sounds fun to me." Kate turned to Marcus. "Do you remember the FBI agent who helped rescue you?"

"In Paris?" Sophie's head bobbed enthusiastically. "Hello."

Marcus pulled out a sparkly gift bag from behind his back. "I brought you a present. I heard you like making paper dolls."

"I do." Sophie's grin widened. "I love them. And I've got lots of presents. Everyone from church, some of our neighbors—"

"Sophie," Kate started. "Remember what your mother said about gifts."

"It's okay." Marcus laughed and handed Sophie

the bag. "Everyone deserves a bit of spoiling every now and then if you ask me. Especially someone who's been as brave as you have."

"Thank you." Sophie beamed up at him.

Marcus winked at her as they stepped inside the house, then shut the door behind them in order to keep out the Texas heat. "You're welcome."

"Is your mommy awake?" Kate asked, looking across the living room. Dora the Explorer sang on the flat screen in the living room. Women from church had come in and transformed the house so that no one could tell what had taken place the day that had changed all their lives.

"Grandma's helping her get ready."

A moment later, Rachel and her mother started down the stairs, while Kate sent up a short prayer, thankful for the simple fact that her sister was alive and beginning to heal both physically and emotionally. Losing Chad would always leave a hole in her heart, but one day, maybe she'd find someone else to help fill that hole.

"I was hoping that was the two of you." Rachel smiled as she made her way slowly down the stairs.

"Marcus, you've already met my mother. This is my sister, Rachel," Kate said as her sister stopped at the bottom of the stairs.

"I'm happy to finally meet you, Rachel," he said, shaking her hand. "Glad to see you up and out of the hospital."

"I'm the one who's happy to meet you," Rachel said. "I owe you so much. You saved my daughter's life."

"And Mrs. Elliot," Marcus said, shaking their mother's hand.

"Please." Kate's mom smiled up at him. "Call me Sharon."

"All right. How are you, Rachel? Kate's been able to keep me updated via Skype."

"I'm tired." Rachel went to the couch, while the rest of them took her lead and sat down with her. "The doctors said I should have a complete recovery. The road there might not always be the easiest, but we're going to make it."

"A lot of prayers have been answered," Kate said.

Sophie jumped up on the couch beside her mother.

"So, Marcus," Rachel said, "I heard you just arrived home from Paris a couple of days ago."

"Took a while to finally wrap up the case, and there will be more involved once the cases go to court, but we've made a total of nine arrests."

Rachel tousled Sophie's hair. "I was hoping for the opportunity to thank you in person for everything you did for me, for Sophie and for Kate."

"You're very welcome."

Rachel leaned forward, her gaze on Kate. "To be honest, I don't want to hear more about the case. What I want to know about is the two of you."

"What about the two of us?" Kate's eyes widened.

They'd taken every chance they could over the past two weeks, between Marcus's investigation and her schoolwork, to talk, making Kate realize what she was discovering with Marcus was worth holding on to. They'd talked about family, work, fears and plans for the future, and in turn, she'd begun to see him as the one she wanted to spend the rest of her life with.

Marcus winked at Kate as she fumbled to answer. "Marcus just got back in town."

"Mom has told me about the late-night Skype calls," Rachel teased.

"The time difference made it a challenge," Kate said.

"Chad and I were married three months after we met." A shadow crossed Rachel's face at the mention of Chad's name. "But while my marriage might not be the best example, don't let it discourage you. Besides, there's something mysterious about Paris when it comes to love."

"As for us," Marcus said, and squeezed Kate's hand, "it might be a bit . . . complicated, but we both think it's a relationship worth working on."

"Look what he got me," Sophie said, pulling out the paper-doll book and smiling up at Marcus. "Will you help me with it later?"

"I would love to, but first I have another present to give out." Marcus smiled at Sophie. "This one is for your aunt Kate."

"Marcus?" Kate's eyes widened.

Marcus reached into his pocket and pulled out a black velvet box, then turned to Kate. "Call me a bit old-fashioned, but since I couldn't ask your father, I decided to ask your mother."

"You asked my mother?" Kate looked at her mother then back to Marcus again. Surely he wasn't . . . proposing . . . now? "You asked her permission to marry me?"

"We went out for coffee," her mother said. "And as far as I'm concerned, you've found yourself quite a catch, Kate. I think you should say yes."

Marcus got down on his knee in front of her and opened up the box. "They're pink amethysts, untraditional, maybe, but diamonds just didn't seem like the right choice. And yes," he rushed on, "I know this is crazy, and fast, but I don't care because I love you and want to spend the rest of my life with you."

Kate covered her mouth with her hand, tears welled in her eyes and her heart felt as if it were about to explode. "I don't know what to say."

"Yes would be the answer I'm looking for."

"Yes . . . yes . . . of course."

He kissed her firmly on the lips until she was certain she was going to melt into a puddle of emotions, while Sophie squealed in the background and her mom and sister clapped and hooted.

"Wow." Kate's heart was still pounding as he slid the ring onto her finger.

"That's just the beginning. I plan to make you very, very happy."

"What else did you have planned?"

"Besides a house in the suburbs and three or four babies?" he asked with a broad smile.

"Three or four?"

"We can talk about that later," he said, grinning. "For the moment, I was thinking dinner with the five of us as a way to celebrate."

Kate couldn't stop smiling. "Are you up to it, Rachel?"

"Absolutely. The doctor said I should try getting out some. Just give us a few minutes to get ready. Someone is still in her pajamas."

"Oh, and there is something else I have planned," he said a moment later when they were alone.

She wrapped her arms around his neck and smiled. "What is that?"

"A honeymoon in Paris. I've always thought you needed to see the city with someone who loves you."

"Paris in the spring is supposed to be beautiful."

"I'm not planning to wait until the spring." He kissed her on the nose, then fully on the lips.

"You're making my head spin," she said.

"I know this has all been fast, but if you have any doubts . . ."

She shook her head. "None. And while it seems crazy, I feel completely at peace. Like you're the missing piece in my life."

"Good, because having you as my wife sounds pretty perfect to me."

Dear Reader,

Like Kate, I have to admit that Paris is one of my favorite places in the world to visit. Along with living in France while attending language school, I have also been able to walk the streets of Paris, and visit the Louvre and the Eiffel Tower a number of times. There is something timeless, romantic and energetic about the infamous City of Lights that I love.

Clearly, though, Kate wasn't in Paris as your typical tourist. While most of us will never have to experience what Kate did, most—if not all of us—will experience a time in our life when we feel as if everything around us is out of control. When we feel propelled down a path we don't want to go.

The words from Isaiah still hold true for us today. "Don't be afraid, for I am with you. Don't be discouraged, for I am your God. I will strengthen you and help you. I will hold you up with my victorious right hand."

Be blessed,

Lisa Harris

ABOUT THE AUTHOR

Lisa Harris is a Christy Award winner and winner of the Best Inspirational Suspense Novel for 2011 from RT Book Reviews. She and her family are missionaries in southern Africa. When she's not working she loves hanging out with her family, cooking different ethnic dishes, photography and heading into the African bush on safari. For more information about her books and life in Africa visit her website at lisaharriswrites.com.

Center Point Large Print
600 Brooks Road / PO Box 1
Thorndike, ME 04986-0001 USA

(207) 568-3717

US & Canada:
1 800 929-9108
www.centerpointlargeprint.com